Praise for

P9-BZH-152

THE FORGOTTEN GIRL

NAACP IMAGE AWARD NOMINEE

ALSC NOTABLE CHILDREN'S BOOK

"This ghost story gave me chill after chill. It will haunt you."
—R.L. Stine, author of Goosebumps

"Engaging, entrancing, and altogether magic! A classic ghost tale that examines racism and segregation in a meaningful story that at its core is about love, friendship, and forgiveness." —J. C. Cervantes, *New York Times* bestselling author of *The Storm Runner*

"A harrowing yet empowering tale reminding us that the past is connected to the present, that every place and every person has a story, and that those stories deserve to be told." —Renée Watson, *New York Times* bestselling author of *Piecing Me Together*

"Scary and spooky and sad and important. I loved every moment of it!" —Ellen Oh, author of *Spirit Hunters* and founder of We Need Diverse Books

"Frightening and mysterious. A new, creepy favorite."
—Dan Poblocki, author of Shadow House and *The Ghost of Graylock*

"The pacing of the plot will surely send a chill through the readers' spines. [An] eerie read." —*Booklist*

"Both historically and culturally relevant, Brown's thoughtful ghost story explores the legacy of racism through segregation."
—*Publishers Weekly*

"The historical information about school desegregation, segregated cemeteries, and the Great Migration are welcome, unique additions. A ghostly tale with a historical twist." —*Kirkus Reviews*

the
FORGOTTEN
GIRL

the
FORGOTTEN
GIRL

INDIA HILL BROWN

Scholastic Inc.

This book was originally published in hardcover by Scholastic Press in 2019.

ISBN 978-1-338-31725-1

10 9 8 7 6 5 4 3 2 1   21 22 23 24 25

Printed in the U.S.A. 40
This edition first printing 2021
Book design by Maeve Norton

FOR LIV AND TONY

CHAPTER 1

Iris's nightmares terrified her.

Especially the ones when she couldn't tell if she was dreaming or not. When she was barely awake but not quite asleep, frozen to her bed. Unable to move as monsters crept from the shadows in her room, walking toward her until she squeezed her eyes shut and hastily thought of a prayer.

"When that happens, the witch is riding your back," Daniel's grandmother Suga would say every time she recounted a dream. "To stop them, you have to put a broom under your bed, so she'll ride that instead and let you go."

Everyone else wrote it off as another one of Suga's old superstitions, but Iris so wished her parents would let her keep a broom under her bed, at least for one night. Instead, she just slept with a night-light, even though she felt too old for that.

Her nightmares were what made her afraid of the dark—well, not exactly afraid. She just didn't like how *unsure* the dark was. The way you had to make your best guess. Was that a person standing over her bed, or was it her lamp? An animal eyeing her or a pile of dirty clothes?

The night-light helped.

And so did the snow.

It snowed just enough here, in the small town of Easaw, North Carolina, and Iris was more enchanted by it than anyone else. She loved the way the sunlight danced on the snow in the daytime. Snow made the light even brighter, playing off it and making its own beauty. Even at night, the snow made the world sparkle as it captured the glow from the streetlights.

Iris jumped out of bed and turned her flashlight on and off three times in the direction of Daniel's bedroom window. This was their signal—if either one of them did it, they needed to meet outside immediately. The signal indicated an emergency. And this was *definitely* an emergency—the first snow of the season! She couldn't miss it.

She didn't make a sound—the only noise to be heard was the blood pounding in her ears, matching her heart's thump. She couldn't contain her excitement. She wouldn't let her stupid fear of the dark stop her. Plus, the snow would help her, brightening the night sky like it always did.

And she was careful—she had made Mama tie her scarf on her hair very securely before bed. Mama thought it was so Iris's braids would stay just as fresh as they were when she left the hair salon earlier that day. And it was partly that, and partly their thing, one last time to bond each evening before Iris went to sleep. But tonight, it was also so the *clink clank* of the colorful beads at the end of her many braids wouldn't make a sound when she went outside. Because she *was*, indeed, going outside.

"Please, Mama!" she'd begged just a couple of hours ago as her parents cleaned the kitchen together, Mrs. Rose washing, Mr. Rose drying and placing the dishes in the cabinet. Vashti was laughing at some baby cartoon on the TV. Iris could see the snow outside had started to fall lightly but slow and steady in that Easaw way. She *had* to go out tonight.

"No," Mrs. Rose said without even turning around, without even considering Iris's request. "It's too late. It'll snow all night and be there waiting for you in the morning, Iris. You'll have all weekend to play."

Iris tried hard to catch her father's eyes, willing him to take her side, like he sometimes did when Iris asked for one more piece of cake, to read one more chapter of her book before bed, or to perform one more impromptu step show with Vashti for their parents.

"Daddy?" she asked. It was a risk, asking Daddy right in front of Mama. But she was desperate.

"You heard your mother," was all he said.

Clenching her fists, concealing her anger well enough for her parents not to see, she walked upstairs to her room, careful not to stomp. Her mother did *not* play about stomping.

She changed into her pajamas, brushed her teeth, and waited for her mama to help her tie her hair up and both her parents to kiss her goodnight. She waited until their laughter at their grown-up TV shows stopped, until she heard their footsteps go into their own bedroom. She waited until the entire house fell into hushed silence to crawl out of bed, flashlight in hand, to look at the snow and wait for Daniel. He *had to* know she'd want to go out tonight.

She was still waiting.

"Come on, Daniel," she mouthed, not even chancing a whisper. Neither of them had cell phones, only tablets, and Iris wasn't allowed to use hers before bed anymore. Mama was convinced that late-night screen time was part of the reason she was having nightmares. Daddy said they'd think about giving Iris a cell phone when she turned thirteen if she kept her grades up. This signal was all they had.

She waved her flashlight back and forth across the branches of the tree in the middle of both of their yards. Still nothing.

She did this twice more, then started to get discouraged. Daniel was *way* more of a rule follower than she was. Iris could go by herself, of course, but it wouldn't be as fun without him.

Just as she contemplated this, she saw a light mimicking her own move across the branches. She grinned. Daniel was coming.

She put on her favorite gray sweatpants and purple puffer jacket over her pajamas and opened her door so slowly it felt like an eternity. She tiptoed down the stairs, praying that they wouldn't creak, that Vashti wouldn't open her door, asking where Iris was going. She walked through the kitchen and out through the back door, her feet crunching in her snow boots. She *loved* that crunch.

Iris saw him immediately—her best friend in the whole wide world. Daniel was standing in the yard between their houses in his black puffer coat, looking around. When he saw Iris, he stood up straighter, trying to look less nervous than she knew he felt.

Daniel wasn't always ready for these adventures with Iris. It usually took some convincing—he'd have an argument ready about things not being safe enough, or worrying their parents. Iris had agreed not to push Daniel to go on too many adventures if he'd just play with her outside during the first snow of the season. So he agreed—reluctantly, of course.

"You ready?" he asked, his breath forming a small cloud in front of him. He pushed his too-big glasses back on his nose with a gloved hand.

Iris grinned.

"Let's go."

She chose the woods behind the houses across the street. There was a clearing right before the woods got too deep, far enough away where they could play without anyone seeing them, close enough that they could run back to their houses quickly. They'd never done this before—their parents told them many times they weren't allowed to go back there—but Iris had seen those woods peeking out behind the houses so many times walking home from school, or walking out her front door.

She knew it was the perfect spot.

They walked across the street and slipped between two houses, one of them being the house with the brightest blinking Christmas lights on the block, loud and colorful ones that put Iris's family's plain white lights to shame. Iris chanced a glance backward on the way, in the direction of her house. The windows were so dark, she wouldn't be able to tell if someone was looking back at her. She hoped her parents wouldn't glance out of them, that the snow would continue to fall all night and cover their tracks, as they edged between the backyards and walked through the line of trees to the big clearing.

There were no more flowers or leaves this time of year; just a wide blanket of snow, getting thicker by the second, and the prickly branches of the trees, curling toward the sky like fingers covered in frosting, sparkling in the night.

The trees arched over Iris and Daniel as if they were looking down, watching them.

Once they got to the clearing, they made the biggest snowballs and threw them at each other, giggling but covering their faces with their hands and scarves so no one could hear them. Covered in snow and out of breath, they dropped down to make snow angels on every inch of clear snow. They made so many, not even one was distinguishable anymore.

Iris stood up and looked at their work. The ground was covered with heads and hands and footprints from their angels. She imagined that they belonged to someone other than her and Daniel, that they were signs of invisible people following them around.

She shook the thought out of her head.

"You can't even see the angels anymore." Iris frowned. She looked around for a fresh patch of snow. Deeper in the woods, she could see a smaller clearing in between the tree trunks, before the woods turned thicker and pitch-black. She squinted, trying to see past that little clearing, but her eyes wouldn't even adjust. The snow fell silently around her, touching her nose, her gloves. The moonlight darkened a bit. The darkness was an odd shade of pink.

Iris knew that straight through these woods was her school, but she'd never bothered to test out the shortcut. Their parents warned them not to go into the woods by themselves. And Suga warned them twice as much about the spirits of the snow. How they preyed on children who wandered out in the snowy darkness alone.

But in that little clearing, there was a fresh, untouched blanket of snow, calling her farther into the woods, just before that impenetrable wall of darkness.

It was *too* dark. The branches looked like spiders, waiting to pull her into the darkness and swallow her whole. Like in one of the nightmares she had last week.

She shook her head again. She was *not* afraid of the dark. And she didn't want to pass up the chance to keep playing.

She pointed a purple-gloved finger deeper into the woods.

"Let's go over there."

Daniel cleared his throat. "Iris, we can't go over there. We shouldn't even be out *here*."

She rolled her eyes.

"It'll just be for a second. I promise." She added, when he frowned at her, "Please? Come on."

He nodded slowly. Iris pulled him farther, past the edge of the big clearing, through the next line of trees, to the smaller one. The darkness seemed so solid as it surrounded them, it felt like they were in a cave. All around her, Iris could only see trees. As if they'd entered another world.

The trees seemed to stand in anticipation under the pink-and-black snowy sky. Watching, waiting, so still as the snow touched the branches. She shivered, probably because of the cold. She lay down slowly, the cold pressing closer against her back than it had before. She moved her arms and legs, making the angel, ignoring a strange feeling that she was slowly sinking into the snow . . .

Daniel reached out his hand and pulled her up. Iris shook the feeling off and smiled. She was proud of her work. "I've never made a snow angel this good!" She looked at Daniel to agree, but he was leaning over, frowning at her angel.

"What's that?" he asked, pointing at it. "Look."

She peered more closely at the angel, the way her dress flared around her feet, her arms frozen in midair as if she'd finally gotten their attention.

There was something buried, just barely, under the snow angel's chest, where her heart would be. It glistened in the moonlight. They bent over and worked together to uncover it.

Their hands froze in midair, mimicking the angels'.

Daniel gasped.

"Iris, that's . . ."

Iris stared down at the crumbling stone, a gust of cold air pushing past her, forcing her to speak.

"A grave."

The wind whistled as they looked down at the marker and the angel surrounding it. She almost looked like she was guarding it. Iris felt the sensation of someone standing behind her, and whipped around just in case. She thought she saw something flicker in the distance, and she forced herself to calm down. It must be one of the twinkling lights from the Christmas house.

Iris shivered. It felt even colder, but surely that was because they had stopped running around.

"What does it say?" she whispered, her voice cutting through the silence. Daniel wiped the falling snow away from his glasses, took a breath, and knelt down by the small gray square. He was shivering, too.

"Avery Moore. Rest in peace, darling. May 5, 1945 to September 7, 1956."

Daniel stared at the grave marker for a second, his lips moving as if he was counting under his breath, then looked up at Iris, his eyes even bigger behind his glasses.

"She was our age."

Iris shivered again. They were silent, both probably thinking the same thing—*what happened to her? Why was she buried here?*

Suddenly, the snow didn't feel fun anymore. It was too dark out. Too cold. Too quiet. They felt too far from their houses.

"I'm cold," they both blurted out at the same time, startling each other. Their voices seemed to carry farther than they should've on the wind.

"Iris, let's go back." Daniel scrambled to stand up and grabbed Iris's hand again, first walking, then running through both clearings. The trees stood tall and dark, ominously, as they passed by. The snow fell heavier, no longer looking like frosting. The white branches were now skeletal hands, waving them backward. Iris could almost feel it, a pull trying to keep them there.

"I'll see you tomorrow," Daniel breathed, before letting her hand go and slipping through the back door to his house. Iris slipped through her own, forgetting to wipe her feet on the mat outside, not so carefully walking up the stairs, and throwing all her wet clothes into her closet. The darkness felt thick, the same way it had by the little clearing. Like it followed her here.

Still shivering, she trained her eyes on her night-light, but the small glow gave her little calm. She began her usual ritual of looking around to prove to herself that the pile of clothes in the corner wasn't an animal, that the *tap-tap-tap* in the window right now was just ice and not someone trying to get her to look up—

But when she glanced at the window, it was into the black, round eyes of a little girl.

CHAPTER 2

Daniel had trouble sleeping that night. He lay in bed, wide-awake, listening to the occasional snore from his grandmother Suga in the room next to his. She slept soundly.

Daniel didn't consider himself brave. Iris was his best friend in the entire world, and she was brave enough for the two of them. But out there in the dark woods, he didn't feel as afraid when they found the grave as someone else might be. He felt afraid to get caught by their parents, of course, and he knew being in the woods at night was kind of dangerous—but he felt no qualms about being in what was probably a graveyard. He might not be brave, but he wasn't afraid of the dead.

He thought about his own dad—he wasn't a ghost, but sometimes when Daniel dreamed, he felt like they were communicating still. When Iris's little sister, Vashti, was younger, she'd smile at random spaces and things. "That's Cecil playing with her," Suga would say when she did that. "Babies can talk to angels, you know." Daniel didn't always entertain Suga's superstitions, but he quite liked that one.

He missed his dad very much. So did his mama. So did Suga. So did everyone. They went to visit his grave every Sunday, or every other Sunday in the wintertime. Suga would only go if it wasn't snowing—another one of her superstitions. Mama and Suga would lay their flowers down and rub the tombstone—so much nicer than the one he saw tonight—and Daniel would just stare. Just taking in the fact that his dad was okay now, and no longer in pain.

Dad would never say that Daniel wasn't brave. "None of the people close to you would say that," Iris told him before, and it was true. Mama said Daniel was very brave at Daddy's funeral, as he greeted the guests and thanked them for coming.

Suga liked Daniel just the way he was, even if she never wanted him to go anywhere, or do anything, out of fear that she'd lose him, too. Just like she lost her own son.

"One day, you'll blink and be the man of the house. But right now, you're just a kid. Don't rush it," his dad had told him. It was one of the last things he'd ever said to him.

Sometimes he'd have dreams of his dad telling Daniel how proud he was, and he'd wake up with a huge grin on his face. They always felt so real.

And Daniel kind of saw what his dad meant—lately he had started to clean his room more frequently and help Mama with the dishes without being asked. But on the other hand, the boys at school were saying he was being a baby. He was slowly but surely losing his interest in basketball and would much rather go straight home or hang out with Iris. He was withdrawn, not wanting to talk with his friends about why he felt sad sometimes—they didn't know what to say anyway. Out of every kid he knew, Daniel was the only one who'd dealt with the loss of a parent.

He felt strange about playing basketball without his dad's pointers. It was their favorite sport. Their special thing. Plus, his mom or Suga would be worried if something happened to him, if he accidentally hurt himself on the court or something. It was best to stay close by and follow the rules.

"You need to grow up," his friends would say when he rushed home instead of hanging out with them sometimes. "You can't be a baby forever."

But he wasn't a baby, or the man of the house. He was just careful. Just a kid.

A kid, like from the tombstone he saw tonight. Who was she? Why was she buried there, of all places, in a deserted spot in the woods? Had she lived around here? What happened to her? He couldn't imagine his dad being buried in a forgotten spot like that. Daniel felt quite sad for her.

These questions and thoughts of himself, Daddy, Mama, and even Suga sitting around a dinner table filled his mind and carried him off to sleep.

CHAPTER 3

"IRIS!"

She jumped straight up, her limbs and reflexes working together again, so fast her head spun. The girl was gone, and she was looking into the concerned face of her mom.

"Did you have another nightmare?" she asked, glancing at the night-light and back at Iris.

"Um...yes," she admitted, looking around the sun-drenched room. She'd thought she'd seen a girl looking at her through the window last night; that wasn't even possible. Her room was on the second story. It was just another one of her dreams.

Everything looked exactly the same as it did when she went to bed the night before, as she expected. Except for one thing.

The window was open.

How?

Her pajamas were soaked with sweat, but she was shivering. Her heart was pounding again.

I must've opened it last night for fresh air, Iris thought. That *had* to be what happened.

"You look like you just saw a ghost," Mama said to her. "And you put your night-light on. You haven't needed that for a few days."

Mama's eyes wandered around her room until she saw Iris's tablet lying on her nightstand. "I told you about watching videos on your tablet so close to bedtime. Come on, Daniel's already downstairs."

"I'll be right down," Iris said, and her mom turned and left. Iris glanced over at the window again.

No one.

"What time is it?"

"Pancake time!"

"What time is it?"

"Pancake time!"

Mr. Rose did his usual Saturday morning call and response for his usual Saturday morning banana pancakes. Iris loved every bit of it, though; she could always count on herself, her mother, Vashti, Daniel, and even sometimes his mom and Suga, to sit around the table on Saturday morning to a big breakfast made by Daddy—banana pancakes, bacon, eggs, and biscuits. His only rule was that they weren't allowed to eat unless they did the Pancake Time song.

Vashti attempted to make a beat on the table with her hands as Daddy came out of the kitchen dancing and carrying stacks of pancakes. Iris joined Vashti in making a beat. But instead of playing off Vashti's rhythm, Iris accidentally banged the edge of a fork and sent it flying onto the floor.

She felt off this morning. She was still jumpy from her nightmare. She often had bad dreams, but last night's was more vivid than ever before.

Last night. Her thoughts kept bringing her back to the grave marker they'd uncovered. She didn't understand why she was so affected by it—in the town of Easaw, there were graveyards, marked and unmarked, everywhere: in the churchyards, in the long stretches of land separating some of the bigger houses . . . She and Daniel visited his father's grave site regularly. It was always somber, but peaceful.

The grave marker they saw last night was different. It had made Iris feel very strange and uneasy. Her stomach was swirling. She didn't even feel hungry.

Mr. Rose placed a plateful of food in front of Iris with a clatter, pulling her out of her thoughts. A little yelp escaped her mouth.

"Iris is afraid of pancakes," Vashti said, laughing.

"Why are you so jumpy, babygirl?" asked her daddy. "I know my pancakes are scary good, but—"

"I'm just . . . nervous about the new combination I'm teaching at step practice next week, that's all," Iris said, trying to avoid her mom's gaze. "It's . . . kind of hard."

"How can the *captain* be nervous?" Vashti said, stuffing a big piece of pancake into her mouth, pointing her fork at Iris. "You have to be the *bravest*. Scaredy-cat."

"I'm not *scared* of anything." Iris frowned, cutting into her own pancakes. She felt her mom looking at her. Iris didn't need her saying anything and letting Vashti know that her big sister still needed to use a night-light.

"You'll be fine, but you need to eat," her mom said. "You'll think a lot better with a full stomach."

"You, too, Daniel. You've barely touched your pancakes. Eat up," Mr. Rose said. Daniel obeyed and picked up his fork, loading a fluffy piece of pancake into his mouth.

And they ate, talking and laughing lazily around the table. Iris's nerves calmed a little as she settled into the familiar taste of the buttery banana pancakes, crispy bacon, and fluffy biscuits. Her appetite came back. She reached to the middle of the table for the last one in the stack, drowning it in maple syrup.

Vashti reached for the syrup right after Iris, but bumped her plate, knocking her own pancake to the floor.

"Oh, Vashti," her mom said, picking up the pancake and taking it to the trash.

"I'm sorry, Mama!" she said, the threat of tears on her face. Iris looked at Daniel to roll her eyes, but he was giving Vashti a sympathetic look.

"It's okay, babygirl. I can whip you up another one," Daddy said.

"No, just . . ." Mama looked around the table. "Iris, let Vashti have that pancake."

Iris looked up, incredulous, her knife midair. "Mama!"

"Iris, do this for your sister," Mama said, flashing Iris a look. "You've already had two pancakes and that was Vashti's only one."

"But you just told me to eat—"

"Iris Michelle."

Iris tried hard not to suck her teeth as she forked her pancake onto Vashti's plate.

"Thank you, Sissy," Vashti said, and reached over to hug her sister. Iris patted her back gingerly.

"Now, isn't that sweet?" Daddy said, looking around the table, a twinkle in his eye. "My girls. I'm doing grilled cheese for lunch, Iris, so you'll have that to look forward to."

After breakfast, Iris was still grumpy and wanted to get some space from Vashti. She asked her mom if she could go to Daniel's house with him. She wanted to talk about what they saw last night, and to tell him about her uneasiness. Was he feeling as weird and jumpy as she was?

"Yes, but bundle up," Mama said. "It's just as cold as it was yesterday."

Iris ran upstairs to her room, where her puffer coat was lying on the floor.

Iris stared at it. *Didn't I put it in the closet last night?*

She shook her head. Probably not. She hadn't been focused on anything but getting out of the woods.

"I had another weird dream last night," Iris breathed, walking outside next to Daniel. Everything looked so much more inviting in the daytime, the whiteness almost blinding, the sun creating sprinkles of rainbow light on the snow. It made last night seem so far away and relaxed Iris's nerves a little.

"What was it about?"

Iris hesitated. Suga always said that you shouldn't tell a bad dream during daylight if you didn't want it to come true. But she had to know if Daniel was feeling the same way.

"After we came back from, you know . . ." Iris didn't want to say too much, since neither of them was supposed to be outside last night. "I had a dream that a girl was staring at me through my window." Iris shivered, wondering if telling her dream under the bright winter sky would make the girl appear again. "Did you feel weird or have any bad dreams last night?"

"No, I feel fine." Daniel frowned. "We shouldn't go back there anyway, Iris. It was way too dark. What if there were animals or something back there?"

"I know." Iris hated to agree. "But—"

Suddenly, Iris stopped in her tracks, her stomach dropping.

"Daniel! What if—what if it was the spirits of the snow?"

Daniel groaned. "Iris, you can't possibly believe that."

Iris shrugged. Another one of Suga's superstitions was about the spirits of the snow. This one was even stranger than her other ones, because none of the other kids at school had heard of it. It wasn't commonly known like "step on the crack, break your mama's back," the one they'd sing when they jumped over the cracks in the sidewalk on the way to school. This made Daniel believe it was something Suga created to keep them from going outside.

"It couldn't have been, right?" Iris went on, trying to convince herself. "The spirits of the snow—they would've taken us right away if they saw us last night in the snow?"

"Maybe they're warning us to never go back," he said, the ghost of a smile playing on his lips.

She glared at him.

"Last night was kind of . . . weird, since we saw a grave and everything," Daniel said, fidgeting with his glasses.

"Hey, that's probably why you dreamed about a girl, Iris. It was just a bad dream."

"Yeah," she muttered, kicking the snow with her boots.

But she couldn't help feeling like it was something more.

They approached Daniel's back door. He reached for the knob.

"*No!* Don't go in there!" Iris heard Suga yell from inside.

Daniel hesitated for a second. Iris looked at him.

Oh no.

What was going on?

Daniel just shook his head as they walked through the back door of his house, through the kitchen, into the living room, where Mrs. Stone sat with Suga. Mrs. Stone was curled up on the couch, typing on her laptop, while Suga yelled at the TV.

"Ugh, so stupid—Oh, hey, babies!"

Where Daniel thought his grandmother was weird and impractical, Iris revered her. She was a little strange with all her superstitions, but Iris always thought they were so interesting, like relics of Suga's past. They had to come from somewhere.

Daniel, though, was slightly embarrassed of Suga. She was also very protective of Daniel, which was understandable, after everything with Daniel's father. But she was still such a peculiar woman.

They each went to hug Suga and Mrs. Stone. She closed her laptop.

"I'm sorry we couldn't make it for pancakes this morning, I had to catch up on work. I'm heading over in a few to talk to your mama, though, Iris." Iris's and Daniel's families were so close, Iris sometimes wished they just all lived in the same house to make things easier. Mrs. Stone looked at Suga. "You should come, too, Suga."

Suga looked outside and frowned. "Now, you know I don't go outside during fresh snowfall! I never go out during fresh snowfall." She crossed her arms. "I'm not too old to be snatched up by the spirits of the snow."

Daniel's mother smiled warmly. "I'm sorry, Suga. How could I forget?"

Iris took her chance. "Suga," she said. "Can you—can you tell me about the spirits of the snow again?" It probably *was* just a bad dream, but Iris wanted to make sure.

Daniel sucked his teeth, then apologized when his mom eyed him for it.

Suga turned her head slowly and stared at Iris for a second too long, and Iris shivered. It seemed like she was
staring straight through her to a time from her past.

"They're the reason that I tell y'all to not play outside in
the snow by yourselves, *especially* at night." Iris struggled
to keep Suga's gaze, not giving anything away about how
they did exactly that last night. "They find children and
take them away with them, never to be seen again."

She told the tale, her voice low and shaky:

> *When you hear the winter wind*
> *that's the sound of their screaming.*
> *That's when you'll know*
> *spirits of the snow*
> *are ready for their feeding.*
> *Wandering children are their prey*
> *lonely in the night.*
> *They take the children in the snow*
> *feeding on their fright.*

"It's better to stay in the house, where you're safe and
sound," Suga concluded matter-of-factly. Daniel nodded
at that.

"But, say you go outside in the snow and they don't take you?" Iris asked, her heart pounding. The wind was whistling last night. Did that mean the spirits had been with them?

Suga laughed, a light little chuckle. "Winter is just beginning, child. Do you think they'd give up after one time?"

Iris's stomach sank.

"Now, don't scare these kids with that talk, Suga!" Daniel's mom said. "I'm headed out now. I'll be back soon!" She walked out, leaving the silence of Suga's words behind her.

They all sat for a second and watched whatever show Suga was watching on TV. She was yelling, groaning, and talking back to the TV. Iris could tell she was embarrassing Daniel.

They both looked at Daniel's grandmother as she drifted off to sleep. She was mumbling, whining. Iris wondered if the spirits of the snow had been after her all these years, and that's why she'd never go outside in the snow again. Maybe the spirits were trying to catch Suga in her dreams.

The thought scared Iris, and Daniel's house was getting much too dark for her liking.

Snow was falling.

Suga was still mumbling.

"Let's go back to my house. Um, I don't want to wake her up," Iris suggested, and Daniel quickly agreed. They walked to the front door and heard a loud *clank*.

Daniel and Iris jumped.

Suga yelled, jolting out of her sleep.

"What was that?" Iris heard her say, not wanting to turn around. Daniel sighed a little under his breath and walked back to the living room.

"Daniel, wait—" Iris began.

"It's just your fork, Suga," Daniel said, picking up the silverware and the empty plate on the table beside it. "I'll put it in the dishwasher for you."

Iris breathed a quick sigh of relief. She was jumpy for no reason. But Suga's face still looked troubled.

"What's wrong?" Iris asked her.

"You know what that means when you drop a fork," Suga said, her voice getting lower.

Iris swallowed "No. What?"

"We'll be getting an unexpected visitor soon."

"I already know what you're going to say," Daniel mumbled as they walked across the lawn. He pushed his glasses up his nose. His cheeks were cold, his deep brown skin concealing his blush. "But the unexpected visitor is *not* one of the spirits of the snow. Suga's always dropping silverware and we haven't had an unexpected visitor yet."

Iris wasn't convinced. What were the odds of Suga saying that to Iris just hours after she played outside in the snow and felt like she brought something home with her?

"Suga's just . . . being Suga," he added, kicking the snow.

"I don't know why you're always so mean to her. You're the only boy in her life now. She just wants to protect you," Iris said, pushing open her own front door. She was greeted by Vashti, who hugged her around her knees.

"I have an idea for your step show, Iris! I made up a step! See?" Vashti did a simple s*tomp clap, stomp clap* beat.

When Daniel applauded her, Iris couldn't help feeling a little jealous.

"That's cool, 'Ti," Daniel said to her sister, giving Vashti a high five that made her blush and giggle. Iris rolled her eyes.

"Iris! I'm glad you're back. Come look at this, quick." Iris, Daniel, and Vashti walked to the living room, where Mrs. Stone and Iris's mother and father were sitting. Her mother had a frown on her face as she watched what looked like the news.

"Yes, Mama?"

"Look. Did you know about this?"

Iris turned to the TV, where she saw footage of her school, Nelson's Pond Middle.

"Hey," Iris said, pointing, but her mom shushed her.

The screen flashed to an auditorium where some kids Iris's age were being handed awards on a stage. Some of them were Iris's classmates.

"The Young Captains Award Ceremony is held to congratulate and honor students who hold some type of leadership position in extracurricular activities around their school . . ." the reporter was saying.

Iris's mom looked at her at the same moment the thought flashed in Iris's head.

"Were you invited, as captain of the step team? Look, there's the captain of the dance team, the captain of the mathletes club . . ."

Iris's stomach sank. "I—I didn't know about it."

"They didn't tell you, did they? I even looked through my phone, my email to see if they told me . . ."

Not again, Iris thought, scrunching up her face in anger. She *hated* this. Everyone, teachers and students, were always "forgetting" to tell her things, to include her.

Just like Heather forgot to invite her to the slumber party she invited every other girl in her class to.

Just like the Beta Club "forgot" to tell her about the group picture that made the front page of the school newspaper.

It was like they didn't want her to be a part of anything.

She knew she was the only Black girl in a lot of her classes, but . . . in elementary school it had been different. No one cared what race she was. She was always treated fairly.

Iris looked at the TV again. Every captain who was representing her school at the Young Captains ceremony was White.

Her mom gave Mrs. Stone a knowing look. "I'm going to the principal's office first thing on Monday morning to hear their explanation for *this*."

Iris knew what the principal would tell her mom. That the email went out to all the parents but somehow hers got "lost." Iris shook the thought out of her mind. She didn't feel like thinking about that right now.

Mama and Mrs. Stone were talking about it animatedly, while Daniel put a hand on Iris's back. "It's okay," he said quietly. "We know you're a great captain. You eat, sleep, and dream step team."

It was still early afternoon when Mrs. Stone and Daniel walked back to their house. Iris was still upset about how she and her step team were forgotten, again. She loved step team and the fun all the girls had together, laughing and teaching one another steps after school. They'd even competed and won awards, and had a huge competition coming up next semester.

Maybe it was an honest mistake, she thought. She did have to spend a lot of time explaining to teachers and other students what the step team actually *was*.

Or maybe, just maybe . . . they didn't want that snooty, stupid school to be associated with her team.

The step team, the Beta Club . . . Iris was a part of things at her school, but when it was time to get recognized for them, she was always forgotten about.

She left her parents downstairs, cuddled up on the couch, flipping through channels in search of Christmas movies, and passed Vashti in her own room upstairs, playing in her dollhouse. She was talking excitedly to her dolls, giving them directions.

"Okay, now stand over there," she heard Vashti say, as if she were talking to a person. Iris scoffed. What was the doll going to do, walk?

But she thought she heard a voice, a different voice saying, "Okay."

She stopped in her tracks.

Get a grip, Iris, she told herself.

She walked into her own room to find her window open.

Again.

Maybe Mama opened it to let some cool air in?

She grabbed her tablet off her dresser and flopped onto her bed, looking again at the Beta Club picture on the front page of the school website. She squinted hard at the picture, trying to imagine herself standing there, the phantom image of a brown girl with beads in her hair.

CHAPTER 4

At school on Monday, Iris's mom dropped her off personally while she went to speak with the principal about the ceremony.

"I'll talk to you about it when you get out of school," Iris's mom said from the driver's seat. Iris just nodded and opened the door.

"Iris."

Iris turned around, her mom's no-nonsense face breaking into a small smile.

"Try not to think about it right now. Okay? Recognition isn't everything. But I'm still going to discuss this with him."

Iris nodded and forced a smile back as her mom pulled off in the direction of the principal's office. She walked toward the building, the brisk air cutting across her face. The snow was turning to slush on the ground, already muddied from the footprints of the other kids who had entered the school before her. She saw the footprints and thought again of the graveyard—how she felt like the hand- and footprints were following her. Maybe one of the spirits of the snow *was* following her.

The wind whistled a bit, causing Iris to shiver, before she opened the door to the main entrance of Nelson's Pond Middle, the small middle school she and Daniel attended. The air was always slightly cooler here because of the breeze that came off the pond behind the school, but Iris couldn't help thinking of the spirits.

> *When you hear the winter wind*
> *that's the sound of their screaming.*

She *had* to get a grip. She shook her thoughts out of her head and rushed to her locker to grab her books.

Iris walked into social studies, one of the only classes she had with Daniel, and took her seat between Daniel and her friend from the step team, Kayla. The class around her was chattering animatedly about something.

"What's going on?" Iris muttered to Daniel, putting a notebook on her desk.

"Nothing," Daniel said. He fiddled with his glasses. "It's not important."

"So, were you nervous?" a classmate behind Iris asked Heather. "You're practically a celebrity now!"

Heather Benson turned around in her desk and smiled, her long blonde hair hitting Daniel in his face. "Not at all! As editor of the school newspaper, I'm used to interviewing and being interviewed. The one difference is, this was actually televised!"

Iris rolled her eyes. Of course. Everyone was talking about the Young Captains feature on the news this weekend.

Kayla looked at Iris. "Why weren't you there?"

The jumpy feeling Iris felt about the footprints outside coupled uncomfortably with a sad pang in the middle of her stomach. Step team was so important to her and to her teammates. This weekend, it felt like it didn't even exist to some people.

"Yeah, Iris, we missed you!" Heather said, flashing a smile. Iris ignored her.

"I wasn't invited. I guess the school forgot to invite me to something *else*," Iris said, an edge to her voice. She was already tired of talking about this. "My mom is talking to the principal now to figure out what happened."

"Oh, I'm sure it was an accident," Heather said. "Did your mom check her email spam folder?"

Iris's emotions were boiling over. "Yeah, like it was an accident that I didn't hear about the Beta Club photo? Miss *Editor of the Newspaper*?" she said, her voice rising.

"Iris," Daniel whispered. He jerked his head to the front door, where the teacher was walking in. The class grew quiet around her.

Heather's cheeks turned pink. "What, you think I left you out of that photo on purpose? Oh, come on. It was an *accident*." She rolled her eyes. "Maybe the Young Captains Society forgot to invite the captain of the step team—or maybe they felt like it was too close to what the dance team does. And dance was already represented."

"Just because you can dance, doesn't mean you can step." Iris sneered. "So you can just—"

"Iris! Settle down, please," Mr. Hammond said.

Iris looked up at the teacher. "But—I wasn't—"

"Iris. Just drop it and settle down."

Iris sighed and opened her notebook. Wasn't Heather going to get called out, too?

It seemed like Iris kept getting remembered for the bad stuff, but never for the good stuff.

Class dragged on in another history lesson she'd heard about a million times until Mr. Hammond handed out a stack of papers to each student.

"A project," Mr. Hammond said. "About getting to know the community you live in, outside of these walls. Easaw is rich with history, with the town dating back to 1869. You never know what you'll find right in your own backyard. I have some ideas that you can choose from, or you can come up with your own. This will be done in groups of two. Pick your partner and get together. Be ready to tell me your choice of topic by the end of class."

Iris and Daniel looked at each other and grinned. A group project with just the two of them would be fun.

Daniel scooted his desk to Iris's and together they looked at the options they could work on for the project.

They were all boring.

Iris read off the list. "The Parks of Easaw...the Agricultural Impact of Easaw ... the Confederate Soldiers of Easaw ..."

"*We're* doing the Confederate Soldiers of Easaw," Heather announced loudly to her partner and the class. "My daddy has my great-great-grandfather's Confederate sword. I already know some of the history!"

"What about the Parades and Festivals of Easaw?" Daniel asked. "That could be fun. I mean, we could talk about the Cornbread Festival since we go every year ..."

Iris scanned the list, again and again. This was all the same stuff she'd learned about ever since second grade. She zoned out, looking around the class at everyone talking excitedly about their projects. Someone was talking about the factories in Easaw, while Kayla and her partner were discussing local sports teams.

She looked out the window; a cloud covered the sun, casting a shadow over the skinny branches outside. It took her back to Friday night, the way the trees looked like they were waiting for her. The branches stretching out, trying to stop her from leaving. She felt that feeling again, that pull. She looked out the window to see the edge of

Nelson's Pond, the light bouncing off the water in the way she loved.

Wait. That's it.

You never know what you'll find right in your own backyard, Mr. Hammond had said.

We could research abandoned graves.

It wasn't a bad idea. She could stop thinking about the nightmare she had about the girl in her window. Prove to herself there were no spirits of the snow after her. Then she could go back to not being afraid of anything.

"Mr. Hammond," Iris said, raising her hand. "So, we *don't* have to pick a topic off of this list?"

Mr. Hammond rubbed his beard. "No. As long as it has historical context in Easaw, you can pick whatever you want."

"Daniel," Iris said, her voice almost a whisper. "Listen. Let's do abandoned graves of Easaw."

Daniel raised his eyebrows. "Why?"

"Because that way, we can find out more about that grave we saw and why that girl was buried out there in the woods, of all places." The thought was knitting together in Iris's head, faster than Suga's fingers when she made those scarves for her and Daniel.

"Iris." Daniel sighed. "Are you still thinking about that?"

"Five more minutes, class," Mr. Hammond said. "Be ready to turn in your topic."

Iris looked at Daniel. Daniel looked down at the suggested topics and shrugged.

"Hmm. It *is* pretty sad that her grave is just back there, forgotten. We could bring some recognition to it. Okay. It beats writing another essay about the Cornbread Festival." He wrote *Abandoned Graves in Easaw* on his paper and circled it.

Iris grinned. Iris and Daniel's project was going to be so different that it was bound to get noticed.

She looked toward the window again, at the trees swaying in the winter wind. The branches looked like old, dead fingers, waving at her.

CHAPTER 5

Iris and Daniel walked home, passing the basketball court where some boys from school were playing. The boys called and waved to catch Daniel's attention, but he pretended he didn't hear them.

"Come on," Daniel said, walking past them a little bit faster, turning his face away. Iris jogged a little to catch up with him.

"Daniel," Iris said. "What's up? Why don't you ever play with them anymore?"

Daniel shrugged, and Iris frowned. She remembered when Daniel would play basketball every day after school, meeting up with her after she finished step practice so they could walk home together. Now, she realized, he never played anymore.

"I just don't. I've been having a lot of homework lately. I need to go home earlier to study."

"Daniel," Iris said again. "Really? I know we don't have all of the same classes, but I think the homework is the same amount—"

"I just don't want to right now, okay? I haven't been in much of a mood to play basketball."

Iris opened her mouth to ask Daniel if it was because basketball was his thing with his dad, but Daniel had an edge to his voice that he didn't normally have, so she decided against it.

They walked in silence for a little while, passing the courts and the adjacent street with all the small local shops. Iris thought back to the one pair in the class doing a project on Easaw's most famous small businesses.

Iris filled the silence by patting her thighs to the rhythm of the new combination she was working on for her step team. They turned onto their street, and Iris stared transfixed at the trees behind their neighbors' houses, the bare branches curling around and up toward the gray sky. She felt that pull again, the same one she felt the other night. With every gust of wind, the branches swung, beckoning her to the clearing.

It was still daytime. The weak sun shone down from

the gray sky. She wasn't afraid. Well, she was never afraid. But especially not right now.

"Hey." Iris stopped abruptly. "We should go back to the clearing and look at that grave again."

Daniel turned to Iris, his brown eyes wide behind his glasses. "Iris, are you serious?"

"For research! We're doing a project on abandoned graves, we might as well research the one we just found in our own neighborhood." The yearning to go back to the clearing was getting stronger. She'd walk straight inside the clearing, right now, if she'd let herself.

"For research, we should start in the library," Daniel said.

"But this is hands-on research, just like when we go outside to look at plants and bugs and . . . stuff."

"Iris, I don't think that's the same thing."

They continued walking, slowly. Iris could almost hear her name in the wind, in the crunch of the snow on the sidewalk, calling her back.

Iris. Iris. Iris.

They paused in front of their houses. Iris felt so strongly that the woods were whispering a secret, and she wanted to know what it was.

It was strange, knowing that a little girl was buried back there. So close to her own bedroom window. She had to know why, to know what happened to her. Maybe that's why she had that dream. And the only way to stop herself from having it again was to face it head-on.

"I'll see you tomorrow, Iris," Daniel said, jerking Iris out of her thoughts. She waved as he walked to his house.

"Hey, baby!" Iris heard the familiar, high-pitched voice of Suga. She peeked her head out and waved. Iris waved back.

Before she went in her house, Iris turned and looked at the trees again. She saw the trees move, but didn't feel any wind against her body. The branches were the only things moving around her. They were beckoning to her, telling her to come back.

CHAPTER 6

The sound of a sports channel murmured through the house, accompanied by her daddy's occasional clap or groan at the TV. The dinner he made and the dessert Mama made sat heavily in Iris's stomach.

Her parents sat on the couch together, and Vashti was in her room, talking, giggling with her dolls.

Iris was in the dining room, slowly putting her school books back in her book bag.

"Oh, Iris, I need to talk to you." Her mom stood up and walked toward her, her lips pursed in a straight line. Iris's stomach lurched. Did she find out about them sneaking to the clearing?

"Yes, Mama?"

Mrs. Rose sighed. "I talked to the principal today about how irresponsible it was that we weren't given notice about the Young Captains Award Ceremony, and that we had to find out on television with everyone else."

"Mm-hmm?" Despite herself, Iris's stomach jumped again, with a little hope. She couldn't help it. Maybe they would honor her again, alone, or make an announcement on the intercom, or—

"He gave the same terrible excuse. That I, along with everyone else, got an email and it must have been in my spam folder. When I assured him it wasn't, he said that he'd send your certificate in the mail."

Iris's heart sank. While announcing her achievement on the intercom wouldn't have been as good as being on TV, this wasn't even close.

"Don't worry, Iris, I let him have it, for the both of us." She gave Iris a hug. "You know what great work you're doing and so does the step team. I don't want you to get caught up in doing things for show. Just keep doing what you're doing. Be so good that they can't ignore you."

Iris just nodded as her mom kissed her on the cheek and said to her father, "I'm going to give Vashti a bath and put her to bed."

"Okay," Daddy grunted, then clapped at the TV. "I'll be right up."

Iris just stood there, watching her dad watching TV, her book bag on her shoulder. She was going to go upstairs, too, but she couldn't ignore how this news made her feel.

Be so good they can't ignore you.

Iris planned to do that. Once the step team competitions started up again next semester, Iris knew her team would be more than ready. But she wanted to do something *now*.

To show Heather and everyone.

Her project on an abandoned grave in her neighborhood would be so much cooler than Heather's great-great-grandfather's Confederate sword. She had to find out more.

She needed to go back.

Iris looked around her house. All the lights were on, including the ones on the Christmas tree, making her house feel safe, warm, and cozy.

She walked behind the couch, through the foyer, to the front door, and looked out of the window beside it. There were the trees, still swaying in the moonlight, so dark compared to the blinking lights on the house in front of them.

What if the spirits of the snow were real, and one caught her this time?

It's okay, she thought. *Don't be scared. It's just research for our project.*

That's all.

She watched Mama walk upstairs, and halfway up, Iris blurted out, "Oh! I left my tablet at Daniel's."

Her mother stopped on the steps. "Oh, Iris. When did you take it over there?"

"Um—today. I stopped by really quickly after school."

She absolutely hated lying to her mom. But she had to go see the grave again. She had to have the best project. She had to prove to herself that she wasn't afraid.

Iris heard a faint giggle.

Her eyes widened, until she realized it was Vashti, of course, her laughter coming all the way down the stairs. Iris fought hard not to roll her eyes again, frustrated at herself for jumping, but also at Vashti. She knew playing with dolls could be fun, but was she really laughing that hard at her own jokes? Vashti was probably doing it to get Iris's attention. Well, she had more important things to do.

"Can I go get it?" she prompted.

Mama looked at Daddy on the couch. "Just wait until—"

"Mama! Daddy!" Vashti yelled. "Are y'all coming?"

Mama looked at the stairs then at Iris.

"Okay. But come *right* back."

Finally, her putting all of her attention on Vashti can help me, Iris thought sadly.

"I will," Iris said.

She had to be quick.

She ran upstairs behind Mama to get her jacket. When she opened her bedroom door, her window was open again, the whistling wind blowing her curtains around.

Again?

It had to be Vashti. She was up here by herself.

She went to the window and quickly did the flashlight signal, hoping Daniel would come with her.

Just in case.

Daniel was lying on his bed when he saw it.

He had been drawing earlier, thinking up ideas of a picture to give to his mother for Christmas, before it got too dark as the sun set behind the house. He just lay there for a second, not getting up to turn on the light in his bedroom.

Then he saw a light outside, turning on and off, on and off, on and off.

The signal from Iris. She wanted him to come outside.

Again? At *night*?

Daniel sucked his teeth. She'd promised that she wouldn't ask him to come out again if he went with her the first time, and look at how horribly that turned out. They ended up making snow angels on top of someone's grave.

She was waiting for his response. *What should he say?*

He didn't want to go, but he didn't think it was safe for Iris to go alone either. That was too complicated to say through flashlight.

Maybe if he could just—

"Daniel?"

He heard his mom's voice, moving smoothly through the dark to his ears.

"Yes, Mama?"

"Are you okay? You went to bed early tonight." The lingering smell of tonight's roast beef and potato dinner reached his nose. He was stuffed. Relaxed. Unwilling to sneak out and risk having his mom come into his room in the middle of the night to find an empty bed, unwilling to let her think she lost another person she loved.

Daniel hoped Iris didn't do the flashlight signal again while his mom was standing there.

"I'm okay, Mama," he said. "I promise."

"Goodnight, I love you so much." She closed the door.

It was settled. He couldn't go, even if he wanted to. He reached under the bed and picked up his flashlight, and turned it on for ten seconds.

The signal for no.

Daniel flashed his light once for ten seconds.

He wasn't coming.

Iris's stomach sank. She knew he probably wouldn't, but she was still keeping her hopes up.

Oh well.

She walked downstairs, shielding the tablet that was already in the pocket of her puffer coat.

"I'll be right back, Daddy," she said to her father. "I'm getting my tablet from Daniel's."

"Okay," he said, not taking his eyes off the TV.

Iris slipped outside, the air cold and thick, the overcast sky an inky blue.

She looked one more time at her house, making sure her mom wasn't peeking out the window.

She wasn't. She was probably too busy with Vashti anyway.

Iris walked, crossing her arms, looking at the line of trees swaying behind the houses.

"Trees talk to each other," Suga once told her. "My aunt was afraid of them. She said she could hear what they were saying."

Iris felt the trees were telling her to come back to the grave.

She answered them, walking with her arms still crossed, the only sounds the crunch of ice and slush beneath her feet.

She walked straight past the houses to the big clearing, without stopping or slowing down.

There were the hand- and footprints she and Daniel had made a few days ago, distorted in the ice, melting into one another, mixing with the mud underneath. The sight made her nauseous.

She walked into the smaller clearing, the darkness falling over her instantly.

Everything seemed sharper around the edges. Stark. The branches of the trees pointier at the ends, the twigs on the ground like worms.

Iris looked at the snow angel she made. While the hand- and footprints were warped, this snow angel was still perfect. An icy snow angel with a grave marker in the middle of her chest.

It was very still. No sound. It felt like the calm before the storm.

She broke that silence when she decided to take a picture of the grave marker with her tablet. They could use it in their project, during their final presentation. She fumbled with the tablet, her gloveless fingers cold as she took a picture of the angel, of Avery Moore's grave. The flash that lit up the snow didn't reach the darkness beyond the clearing.

Tsst.

She whirled around, hearing something that sounded like a twig snapping.

She had the sudden, overwhelming feeling that someone was right behind her, about to tap her shoulder.

Suga said if you looked over your left shoulder and saw a ghost, it was probably the devil. If you looked over your right, it was likely an angel. Iris had no intentions of looking over her left shoulder.

She turned her head ever so slightly to the right, looking out of her peripheral vision.

Nothing.

As much as Iris had felt drawn into this clearing, she now wanted to run away, straight back into the house, into her bed, with her night-light. But she was already here. She wished Daniel was, too.

She looked at the gravestone again.

Avery Moore.

She studied it, ran her fingers over it, got on her hands and knees and started scraping snow, twigs, dirt away.

She kept going, clearing the area of snow, the frozen earth hard and cold under her nails.

Her left hand hit something. She grabbed a fistful of dirt and tugged it up, seeing a crumbling block.

Another gravestone.

There was a small glass pane in the middle with words scribbled on it in pen. Iris couldn't make out the name. It looked like it could've said *HENRY*, but she could make out the years: 1915–1950.

"Wow," Iris mouthed, the cloud of heat lingering too long in front of her mouth before fading away.

Iris dug and dug, grabbing for answers, even using her foot to take up dirt and slush.

Every so often, her hand hit something else solid.

Iris kept digging, holes all around her.

She'd uncovered five grave markers.

She was sitting in the middle of a graveyard.

CHAPTER 7

Iris thought of all the bodies under her.

Something cold hit her nose.

Snow.

Oh no.

> *They take the children in the snow*
> *feeding on their fright.*

A cold gush of air washed over Iris like a bucket of water.

The spirits of the snow were coming for her. Iris should've never come here by herself.

Something was behind her.

Don't look, don't look, Iris willed herself, but the urge was too strong.

She could feel a presence.

But instead of body heat, she felt cold air.

She peeked around her right shoulder, held in her shriek.

There was a little girl, standing with her back to Iris.

"Hello?" Iris said.

She didn't answer.

She wore a light dress that didn't even cover her bare legs, but she kept completely still despite the harsh cold.

What was this girl doing out here? Had she come from one of the neighbors' houses?

"Hello?" Iris repeated.

The girl slowly turned around; her eyes were black holes, swallowing the moonlight. She was smiling, but unmoving.

This was the same girl Iris saw in her dream.

She couldn't be real. Was Iris dreaming again?

But she wasn't in her bed, she was outside.

Iris saw straight through the girl to the trees behind her. Iris backed up slowly, and her foot slipped on the icy snow angel, pulling Iris down to the grave.

She felt frozen to her spot.

Was this girl a spirit of the snow?

Iris whimpered. If she fed off of fright, she'd feast on Iris, right there. She was going to be eaten in the snow by this spirit and her family thought she was at Daniel's, getting her tablet. They wouldn't even know where she went. They were probably playing with Vashti, reading her stories.

She needed to do something, be brave, so that the spirit couldn't feed off of her fright.

Forget this, Iris thought.

Instead, she made a run for it. She ran as fast as she could, trying to avoid the girl.

Iris slipped on the ice again and fell facedown.

She scrambled up, turned around to see where the girl was.

The girl vanished into thin air, turning into branches and twigs and tree trunks and nothing at all.

She was there and then gone, just like in the dream.

Iris didn't hesitate. She slipped again as she exited the little clearing, the big clearing, crossed the street, ran to her house.

She dashed through the front door and slammed it behind her. Iris let the door block out the fear and dread and terror, and let the warmth of her familiar home wash over her.

Daddy glanced at her and smiled before turning his attention back to the TV.

A noise came from the kitchen.

Iris jumped. "What was—"

"Iris, your sister wanted to tell you goodnight." It was Mama yelling from the kitchen, pouring herself something to drink. She heard the clinks of glasses, the flow of liquid. "She just lay down not too long ago."

"Okay, I'm going upstairs now." Iris sprinted up, to get as far away from the front door as possible.

She was imagining things. She dreamed about the girl before, and she was in a dark and scary place and had been thinking about her again. *You were thinking about Suga's story, that's all*, Iris told herself, her feet thudding on the stairs. She still couldn't shake the feeling of something dark behind her.

She heard her sister, giggling softly, talking in her room. She threw the door open, the only light coming from Vashti's night-light.

"What are you laughing at? Who are you talking to?" Iris asked frantically.

There was a shadow of a girl on the wall.

Iris jumped backward out of the room, then realized it was one of Vashti's dolls on the floor, causing a distorted silhouette.

"My friend," Vashti said. Iris could hear the grin in her voice.

Iris tried to calm her pounding heart. She looked at the doll, a smile frozen on its face.

"Your friend?"

"Yes. Do you want to meet her?"

Stop. Vashti always did this. She loved her dolls. Iris wouldn't let herself think anything else.

"No. It's getting late. Goodnight."

"Goodnight, Sissy."

Iris gave her sister a kiss on her forehead before leaving the room. Vashti's skin was cool to the touch.

Calm down, Iris, she told herself.

Her mind was playing tricks on her, with what she saw . . . it was kind of scary, being out there alone in a graveyard. Of course she'd think she saw a ghost in the trees.

An entire graveyard. Right in their neighborhood. They could focus in on it for their project and find out why it was back there, unmarked. Why all those graves were back there. Forgotten about. She shivered as she thought of herself out there, standing on top of them.

She hastily changed into a pair of pajama pants with snowflakes whirling all around them, and an old step team shirt. She turned on her night-light and pulled the covers high over her head.

Tap-tap-tap.

The tree branches played their eerie song on her window, and Iris squeezed her eyes shut and prayed the spirits of the snow wouldn't come for her tonight in her dreams.

CHAPTER 8

"There were at least five grave markers out there!" Iris whispered-shouted. She'd been trying to tell Daniel this story all day, but they had a test in social studies, and by the time they got their lunch in the cafeteria, the period was basically over.

Now it was the end of the school day and they were in the school library, doing research for their project and recapping the strange events from the night before.

"Daniel, we're walking distance from a graveyard that we didn't even know existed!"

"That's what our project is for," Daniel said, logging on to the school computer, pushing up his glasses. "We can find out why those graves are abandoned back there, but in the safety of the library."

Iris wanted to know why there was a graveyard in her neighborhood that no one knew about, eerie nightmares aside. She wanted to know why all those people had been forgotten about.

She went to the Web browser and typed in one of the few legible names on any of the graves back there.

Avery Moore, Easaw, NC.

Nothing popped up.

She tried again, including the date and their neighborhood.

Still nothing.

It was like there was no trace of this girl. But she knew she'd lived. Along with all those other people who had graves.

Maybe the spirits of the snow killed her.

Maybe the spirits killed them all.

She'd searched for *spirits of the snow* in vain, knowing that Suga's legend wouldn't come up. Although there were tales of winter spirits in different cultures, she didn't find one that fit Suga's tale. She didn't tell Daniel, knowing he would tell her "I told you so."

She searched again, typing in the name of their neighborhood and *graves*. The only thing that came up that time was Sampson's Perpetual Care, where Daniel's father was buried.

"Daniel," Iris said. "Why is there *no* mention of that grave—or any grave in our neighborhood—online? Look—that Avery girl's name is not even coming up!"

"Hmm." Daniel shrugged. "That could be a good thing to talk about in our slideshow for the project."

She tried again, searching *abandoned graveyards in Easaw, NC.*

After scrolling through a few websites, she found a very old, very plain website with a gray background and a black-and-white picture of woods with a single headstone peeking through the trees.

Iris shivered. It wasn't their neighborhood, but this graveyard looked similar.

There are many reasons for unmarked or abandoned grave-yards, the website stated, *one of the most common being segregation, which occurred even after death. Some segregation occurred in the form of a single, divided cemetery—when this was the case, there were two sets of caretakers to look after their respective races, with Whites usually getting the more attractive plots. There was also the practice of having completely separate cemeteries. As communities changed, especially through the Great Migration when African Americans fled the Jim Crow South to move to Northern cities, the cemeteries solely for African*

Americans or the African American spaces in cemeteries were left
untended, overgrown, and eventually forgotten.

Iris was immediately transported back to a conversation her mom once had with Mrs. Stone, about how the neighborhood they lived in was once predominately Black.

It clicked.

No wonder she felt so strange in that graveyard. No wonder the trees swayed, begging for her attention. They were trying to be noticed. Trying to draw attention to the forgotten lives back there.

The thought made the hair on her neck stand up. She was upset about being forgotten by the principal, but she couldn't even imagine being forgotten in a way like this. That was almost scarier than being in the dark.

"Daniel!" she whisper-shouted again. "This graveyard probably wasn't just abandoned. It was probably *segregated*, too. Think about it." She passed him her tablet.

Daniel skimmed the page and then looked at Iris, deep thought and sorrow washing over his face.

"You're probably right. That's so sad."

"But we can help them!" Iris's thoughts were turning a mile a minute. "With our project, we can bring recognition to the people buried there! Instead of talking about graves, we can focus our project on segregated graveyards!"

They could have the best project and do something good at the same time. Iris's stomach did flips. She *knew* there was a reason she went back.

"Hey," Iris said thoughtfully, "do you think our parents know anything about this?"

"Maybe," Daniel said. "But how can we ask them about this graveyard without revealing that we snuck out? I don't want to get in trouble."

Iris tapped her finger on her chin.

"I'll take the heat."

"Iris—"

"Come on, it's okay. It's just more research, remember? And you'll owe me one."

Daniel sighed at his friend, but gave her a small smile that Iris returned shakily. They were one step closer to having a great project and figuring out what was up with that graveyard, but Iris couldn't shake that feeling of dread that followed her to school that morning.

"What was the Avery girl's last name again? Moore?" Daniel typed and frowned. "*Avery Moore ... Easaw ...* Hmm. Her name didn't pop up."

"I know. Hey, maybe there was some more information about her on her grave. I took a picture of it last night."

Iris pulled out her tablet and scrolled to the pictures she took last night in the clearing.

She dropped it with a loud *clunk*, and an even louder gasp.

"Do you see that? What is that?"

She pointed to the picture of Avery Moore's grave, the snow angel sparkling all around it. In the back corner of the picture, near the darkest part of the woods, was a dark, smudgy shadow.

To Iris, it looked like a girl.

Her senses were on edge.

She heard every page turn, every door close, every footstep in the library.

She shivered, watching Daniel with wide eyes as he looked at the picture.

He paused while taking a pencil out of his book bag. He licked his finger and tried to wipe the smudge off, like it was a smear on the glass.

It didn't budge.

"Daniel! I thought it was my imagination, but I think I saw a little girl out there. The same one I dreamed about. That's probably her! What if she was real?"

The thought chilled her, the hairs on her arms standing straight up. She rubbed them, her own fingers feeling foreign and cold.

"If it was the same girl you dreamed about, you're probably imagining her again. Or what if it was a real person, watching you?"

It reminded Iris of what Suga once told them. "Sometimes, the living is more scary than the dead."

She looked at the picture one more time, trying to make out what that smudge was.

"There's something going on back there, Daniel."

They had to dig deeper.

CHAPTER 9

"Mama."

Iris was trying to get her attention but she was still talking to Vashti. She'd come home from school on Friday to find her little sister in an almost identical hairstyle to hers, and she wasn't happy about it.

They were at the table, eating a big dinner of lasagna, garlic bread, and salad that Daddy made. Daniel and his mom came this time, too, but Suga had stayed home, as there was fresh snow on the ground. Iris couldn't blame her. She felt like the witch that rode her back, the spirits of the snow, the girl with black holes for eyes, and the dead buried across the street were all among them tonight. The feeling of dread was so strong, dark, and solid behind her, she could practically touch it. Like something would jump out and grab her at any second.

Daniel kept his head down, eating, but looked up and over his glasses at Iris, willing her not to say anything about them visiting the graveyard.

They'd been doing research all week, but Iris couldn't wait any longer. She had to ask her parents.

"Daniel, are you having trouble cutting the lasagna?" Mr. Rose said. "Here, it's easier if you place your pointer finger over your fork. See?"

Daniel did as Mr. Rose suggested.

"Thanks, Mr. Rose," he said, glancing at Iris again.

"Mama," Iris said again. She was talking to Mrs. Stone now.

"Mama."

Mama and Mrs. Stone turned to look at Iris. Mama gave Iris a look.

"Now, Iris. Was that polite to interrupt the grown-ups talking?"

Well, I was trying to get your attention when you were talking to Vashti, but you didn't listen! Iris thought, but instead said:

"I'm sorry. I need to talk to you about something. It's important."

The table got quiet, with even Daddy slowing up on how fast he was eating his lasagna.

"Have you ever heard about a girl named Avery Moore? Or a Moore family?"

"Avery Moore?" Mama scrunched her brow. "No, who is she?"

"I—" Iris didn't want to say it, but she had to. How else would she find out if her parents knew something?

"Avery Moore. Hmm. It sounds familiar," said Mrs. Stone thoughtfully, and Iris perked up.

"Are you sure you aren't thinking of Avery Jones? The actress?" Mrs. Rose asked the both of them.

"Oh, you know what, that's exactly who I'm thinking of," said Mrs. Stone, and Iris's eyes dropped in disappointment.

"Why, Iris?" her mom pressed. "Who is she?"

"Okay, so . . . you know how Daniel and I are doing the project on abandoned graveyards around this town, right?"

"Yes, sweetie."

"Okay. Well . . ." Iris looked at Daniel, his eyes wide under his glasses. "We . . . found one. And we think it might've been segregated. And we've changed the project to focus specifically on segregated sites."

"A cemetery?" her mom asked, glancing at Mrs. Stone. "Where?"

"Yes, ma'am. Um . . ." She paused. Once she said it, there was no turning back.

"It's across the street. In those woods, back behind those houses? There's a clearing back there and . . . I saw it."

Everyone at the table was silent. Even Vashti, who picked up on the fact that something serious had happened, froze with her fork in midair, her beads swinging from side to side.

"There's a girl's grave back there. Her name was Avery and she was around our age. There are others, too, but the names are so old and almost worn off. Daniel and I looked online and couldn't find anything, so we just wanted to know if . . . you . . . knew . . ." Iris trailed off.

Her mom just stared at her, trying to figure out if Iris should be reprimanded or congratulated, in private or in public, right now or later.

"What?" was all she said.

"And I—" Daniel opened his mouth, but Iris talked over him. There wasn't any point of both of them being grounded, or something. Like she said, he could pay her back for it later.

"Yes, Mama." she said. "I went looking, coming home from school one day, because I had a . . . feeling that one was back there." She couldn't tell her mama she'd been sneaking out to do it. She'd never see daylight or her step team again.

"An abandoned cemetery," Daddy said, sighing and leaning back in his seat. "Here. In our own neighborhood."

"And to think, we've been living across the street from it for this long and had no idea . . . Iris, are you sure? It wasn't a—stone or something?"

"I'm sure, Mama," Iris said. "I'm very positive."

"Now, Iris, you shouldn't have gone back there by yourself," Daddy said. "You don't know what else could've been back there."

"I went, too, Mr. Rose," Daniel blurted out before Iris could stop him, looking from Mr. Rose to Mrs. Stone. "I'm sorry, Mama."

Iris's eyes widened in shock. But Daniel *was* a rule follower. He wasn't going to keep this away from his mom if he could help it. And he wasn't a liar. Neither was Iris.

Until recently.

"Daniel!" Mrs. Stone said, her voice high-pitched. "If something were to happen to you back there . . ."

The unspoken words filled the air, and Iris felt a pang in her stomach. Daniel was all Mrs. Stone had; of course she didn't want to lose him.

"We're really sorry," Daniel said. "We won't go back. We're just really passionate about this project."

"Yeah," Iris agreed. "We're sorry."

But Mrs. Rose's face became solemn. "Do not go back there by yourselves anymore. Do you hear me? You don't know what could be lurking back there. Any*thing* or any*one* could be lurking in those woods. It's dangerous. Just do your research and let us know if you need help. Do you understand?"

Iris nodded; she understood more than her mom knew. She rubbed the back of her neck, trying and failing to push away the feeling that something was breathing on it.

"And that goes for you, too, Daniel," Mrs. Stone said. "I don't want to hear anything about you going back there looking for trouble."

"We won't," Iris and Daniel said in unison.

"We're serious," Daddy said, his voice rising in warning.

"We won't," Iris said again, her lie thick on her tongue. She knew she'd be going back. One way or another.

"Good. Now, what else do you plan to do for this project? How did you come to the conclusion that it was segregated?"

Iris put her fork down, relishing the fact that all eyes were on her, not on whatever cutesy thing Vashti was doing.

"Remember how you told us this neighborhood was once predominately Black, Mama? But get this—Sampson's Perpetual Care was a Whites-only cemetery!" The adults gasped. Sampson's Perpetual Care was where Daniel's own father was buried. "When we searched for predominately Black cemeteries in the area, nothing popped up. But they had to be buried *somewhere*, right?" Daniel nodded as Iris spoke, his cheeks full from the lasagna. "So, we think some people were buried back there, in an abandoned graveyard. We're going to keep researching the history of segregation and segregated graveyards in North Carolina . . . and Easaw. When we present our project, we're also going to present some ways that we can get the graveyard restored!"

Iris was practically beaming when she finished. It was almost enough to quell her dread completely.

"I am so proud of you!" Mama exclaimed. "And you, too, Daniel! What a wonderful thing y'all are doing for the community."

Iris just smiled at everyone at the table, even Vashti. Her little sister gave her a cheesy grin in return, tomato sauce all over her face.

"All right," Daddy said. "Now, let's get back to this lasagna."

"Iris," Mrs. Rose said. She was cleaning up the kitchen while Iris's father packed up the leftovers for tomorrow. "I'll be upstairs in a second to help you wrap your hair."

"Mine, too! Right, Mama?" Vashti said, her new beaded hairstyle swinging behind her.

Iris shielded her eye roll from her mother. Beaded braids were Iris's thing—she was the only girl in most of her classes to have them, and Vashti usually wore pony-tails with ball-shaped bows on the end. Now, for some reason, she had her hair just like Iris's and everybody thought it was cute. She already had Iris's old toys and what used to be Iris's second helping of pancakes. Now her hairstyle?

"Yes, sweetie. Actually, I need to do yours first," she said. "Iris, I'll be in your room after I wrap Vashti's."

Ugh. "Okay, Mama. I'm going upstairs."

"Goodnight, babygirl." Daddy came over to give Iris a kiss. "Have a good night's sleep."

"I will," Iris said, her shoulders heavy from the weight of the day. She was ready to call it a night.

She went upstairs and waited for Mama, first reading a chapter of her library book, then picking up her tablet and returning to the photo she'd taken.

Iris stared at the smudge, trying to figure out what she was looking at.

Her door creaked open.

Iris jumped up, but it was just her mother. She quickly stuffed her tablet under her pillow.

"Uh-uh, Iris," her mom said. "Didn't I tell you no tablet before bed? If I catch you again, I'll take it away."

"I'm sorry." Iris took the tablet from under her pillow and put it in the drawer of her nightstand.

"How are you feeling?" Mama asked. "About what the principal and I discussed?"

Iris shrugged. It bothered her, but she didn't feel like talking about it.

"It's fine," Iris lied. "Are you ready to wrap my hair for me?" She reached for her favorite purple scarf.

"Oh, that's what I meant to ask you about—this bonnet is too big for Vashti's head. Can she use your scarf tonight and you use this bonnet?" Iris's mom held up an ugly-looking black bonnet with white and silver flowers.

Iris scrunched up her face. "Ew, Mama."

"It's just for one night. We'll have to get her a new one tomorrow." She walked over to Iris and took the scarf from her hand, replacing it with the ugly bonnet.

My favorite scarf.

As if she read Iris's thoughts, her mama kissed her forehead. "She just wants to be like her big sister, sweetie."

"Hmph."

"I'll be right back. And don't let me catch you with that tablet again."

"You won't," Iris said as her mom closed the door,

leaving her with a darkness that only the night-light cut through.

Iris looked at the bonnet again and tossed it in frustration.

I guess I could say my prayers or something before Mama comes back . . . she thought.

She closed her eyes and folded her hands.

She opened one eye. She felt like someone was staring at her.

There was a *tap-tap-tap* at her window.

She squeezed her eyes shut, and kept them closed until she drifted off to sleep.

Iris's eyes popped open.

She'd heard something.

What was that?

She stared straight at the ceiling, realizing she'd fallen asleep praying and rolled over. Was she still asleep and dreaming?

The door creaked in the darkness.

Iris tried to sit up, but couldn't move.

Oh no, she thought. A nightmare. The witch was riding her back again. Suga told her never to fall asleep on her back—that's how it happens. Now Iris was trapped, forced to look at whatever scary image her mind would make up.

She heard the creak again.

Her heart pounded.

Mama? Had she come back to help her wrap her hair?

She moved her eyes to her bedroom door.

It was still closed.

A movement in the corner of her eye caught her attention.

It was her window, slowly opening with nothing but darkness behind it.

What's going on? Iris thought frantically. She felt helpless. She tried to will herself to wake up from the dream. But she couldn't escape it.

The window slowly slid open more, the darkness behind it threatening to swallow her whole.

The overwhelming feeling of someone being in the room with her took over, as if darkness had climbed into the bed with her.

She couldn't see; the night-light was powerless against the darkness pushing in, reaching for it, swallowing it—

Her night-light flickered, then went out.

Iris was in complete darkness.

She shivered, but couldn't tell if it was from her fear or how cold her room had gotten all of a sudden.

The spirits of the snow.

They were here, finally catching Iris alone and unable to move, feeding off her fright. They would take her back into the snow with them.

Iris wanted to cry, wanted to scream, but she couldn't.

"Iris."

Goose bumps prickled her skin. Cold sweat slid down her forehead into her hair.

She had no choice but to peer into the darkness that pressed in all around her.

Then she saw it.

The shimmering, gray shadow of a young girl emerging from her window, a deeper darkness sitting where her eyes should be.

"Help me," the girl said, her voice too high-pitched. It sounded like one of Vashti's dolls had come to life.

Iris willed her feet to move, her mouth to open so she

could scream for help before the spirit took her back to the woods.

"I'm not here to hurt you," she said, moving soundlessly toward Iris. "I am lost and you found me. You lay on my grave. Your angel rests where I do. You noticed me."

Finally, Iris was able to speak. "Are you—" Her voice cracked. "Are you going to take me away?"

The girl smiled, almost as if she could see through Iris's skull to her innermost thoughts. It was an odd smile that moved as slow as molasses and took over her entire face.

"No, Iris Rose, I only want to be your friend."

Iris stared at the spirit, fear and confusion fighting in her mind. She blinked.

The spirit twirled in a slow circle, her pink dress floating around her like a mist, her skinny legs bare underneath it. She looked young, innocent even, until you saw her eyes.

"Iris, I just want to be your friend."

And the spirit was gone, but her voice still echoed around the room.

"Iris, Iris. Do you know what it feels like to be forgotten? Remember me."

The sun came into Iris's room, gray, watery.

The sound of a door creaking made Iris bolt up in bed. The window was open, the room covered in a thin layer of frost.

"Good morning, Iris."

Iris whipped her head around.

It was Mama, walking through the bedroom door, bringing with her the bright light from the hall and a gust of warmth. All the frost that had covered every surface evaporated in an instant.

Iris rubbed her eyes. She must have still been half asleep.

"Oh, Iris, your braids are so frizzy. Have you been sweating?"

"Mama," Iris said slowly, her heartbeat slowing down, the fear of her latest dream disappearing, replaced with annoyance. "You forgot to help me wrap my hair last night."

She was reminded of the question the spirit asked her last night.

"Do you know what it feels like to be forgotten?"

Mama put a hand to her head. "I did, Iris. I'm so sorry. But . . . you had the bonnet. You could've at least put it on yourself."

Iris said nothing. When Mama wrapped her hair, she kissed her forehead, talked to her, and told her goodnight. It was more than just putting on a bonnet.

Mama grabbed Iris's hand. Her fingers were warm where Iris's were cold and clammy.

"I'm sorry. I won't forget tonight."

"Okay."

"I can fix your hair a little before we leave for church. It's time to get up."

"Okay."

Iris's mother walked out of the room, the gray morning sky opening up to bright sun rays slicing across the walls.

Iris lay there, thinking about her dream last night, how terrified she felt. How *cold* she felt. These dreams were getting more and more realistic.

But at the same time, they weren't making sense. She dreamed about a spirit of the snow that told her she'd wanted to be her *friend*.

It wasn't at all what Iris pictured a spirit of the snow would look like. She just looked like . . .

A little girl.

The same little girl she saw when she was taking a picture of . . .

It couldn't be.

"Your angel rests where I do," the girl had said.

Iris had a feeling she wasn't dreaming about the spirits of the snow at all. She was just dreaming about . . . a spirit.

The spirit of Avery Moore.

Her heart thumped as the realization hit her. Her nightmares hadn't seemed so intense, so realistic, until the night when she'd seen the girl—Avery—in her window. The night after she'd uncovered her grave. That's where the nightmares were coming from. She needed to find out more about Avery. No fear, no nightmares. Just solving the mysteries of who this girl had been when she was alive and why she was so alone in death.

Iris jumped up, following her mama out of her bedroom. It *had* just been another nightmare, right? Even if they were . . . starting to feel more real.

Still, she did not want to be left in her room alone.

CHAPTER 10

It was Sunday morning, time for church. Daniel, his mom, and Suga were all in their rooms getting dressed, Daniel tying his tie exactly the way his daddy taught him.

"Daniel! We're ready!" His mom called him from downstairs.

He looked in the mirror one more time, eyeing the mini waves in his shiny black hair. He bounced down the stairs, his dress shoes slapping on each step. They didn't always dress up for church on Sundays, but they did on days when they knew they'd be visiting Daddy's grave. Daniel wanted him to see how nicely he could tie his tie now.

"Look at my boy, so handsome," Mama said, giving him a kiss on his forehead. Daniel could feel the stickiness of her lipstick still there. "Isn't he, Suga?"

Suga stared at Daniel for a long while. Then her golden-brown chin, surrounded by small lines like the ones on top of peanut butter cookies, trembled as she smiled. "Looking more like Cecil each and every day."

Daniel smiled at both of them. When Suga was like this, she wasn't so bad. "Thank you. And you ladies look beautiful."

Together, the three of them walked to church, which wasn't too far from their house. There were a few flurries last night, but luckily, nothing stuck overnight, so Suga could come, too. Iris and her family usually arrived late, after the congregation finished praise and worship and were all being seated, the Roses whispering and apologizing the whole way down the aisle until they took their seats beside the Stones.

Today was no different, as Iris slid in beside Daniel on the pew behind their parents and Vashti. Vashti tried to sit with them one day, but she was too rowdy without her parents' close eyes, crawling under the seat and laughing too loudly. Daniel knew Iris was relieved when Mrs. Rose told Vashti she couldn't sit there anymore.

The pastor talked about the importance of helping those in need, talking about some of the community service drives they were holding, when Iris nudged Daniel's knee and handed him a note, written on a church program.

I need to tell you something.

Daniel looked at Iris, a question in his eyes. She shook her head and mouthed "Later."

Afterward, when they prayed their benediction and all the grown-ups stood around and talked to one another, Iris pulled Daniel to the back of the chapel, behind the last pew.

"Last night, I thought I was having another nightmare about the spirits of the snow. It was the same girl I thought I saw in the clearing, and in my window . . . Daniel, I think it was Avery Moore. In my dream, she even said, 'Your angel rests where I do,' like, the snow angel I made on her grave."

"Iris—" Daniel started, but Iris stopped him, shaking his shoulders.

"Listen! At first I thought it was the witch riding my back, but this was a different kind of dream. It even *felt* cold in my room. I felt my bed, felt my sweat . . . and every time I see her open the window in my dream, it's really open when I wake up. Something *really* weird is going on around here."

"What?"

"Daniel! I'm not lying! I'm in church! Look, I don't know what happened in the clearing that night, but I think there's a reason I keep dreaming about her. I need to find out more about her to figure it out."

Daniel sighed, exasperated. He *knew* they shouldn't have gone there that night. Iris already had nightmares and now they were worse, probably from guilt and knowing that they played in a graveyard. He didn't think his friend wanted to admit that she was scared. He wanted to tell her it was okay.

"In the dream, she kept saying she didn't want to be forgotten. We need to find out if there are any Moores in the area—" Iris began again, but he looked up and signaled to Iris that their families were walking up, right behind her.

"Come on, Iris, we're going to Eggs Over Easaw for brunch," Mrs. Rose said. She turned to Daniel's mom. "And you're sure y'all don't want us to save you some seats?"

Mrs. Stone shook her head no. "We're going to visit Cecil today, and I need to get home and get some things done around the house; there's a big load of laundry waiting for me."

"On a Sunday?" Suga asked incredulously. "You're never supposed to wash clothes on a *Sunday*."

Daniel scrunched up his face. *Here she goes again with her strange rules.*

"The sermon was beautiful today, wasn't it?" she continued on. "I loved that. Such helpful, nice people here. Danny, do you know when I was your age, Black people weren't even allowed to sit on the front pews like we do here? We had to sit in the back or in the balcony."

"Really?" Daniel asked, suddenly feeling sad. He pictured Suga as a girl, trying to see the pastor from a seat too far away.

"Yup. And the front was reserved for Whites only."

"That's not fair. How can you be mean like that? And in church, too," Iris said, crossing her arms even tighter. She looked at Suga. "Suga, Daniel and I are actually doing a project that deals with segregation in Easaw. Maybe you can tell us more about the things you saw."

Daniel was stuck in between wishing Iris didn't ask, and feeling guilty that he didn't ask himself.

Suga smiled at Iris. "Of course I could, sweetie. Anything to help."

"I can't wait to see the finished product," Mr. Rose said. "It's such an interesting topic—I'm sure the teachers will be talking about it for days."

Iris beamed. Daniel even had to smile, thinking of the look Heather Benson would have on her face. Maybe she'd finally stop hitting him with her hair every time she turned around.

"I think it's a great idea," Mrs. Rose said. "Maybe we can set up a time for y'all to talk this week. But for right now, we have a reservation to make."

Daniel, Suga, and Mrs. Stone walked around the corner and down two blocks to Sampson's Perpetual Care. The sky was overcast, the snow turned to slush on the ground. It was bright and gloomy at the same time.

They walked the usual winding path, cutting through the grass that was so green in the summertime, to the slick, black slab of marble on the ground.

Cecil Stone
Husband | Son | Father

Daniel remembered the first time they came here, after the funeral. His mom and Suga were screaming like he'd never seen them before, like babies throwing a temper tantrum. He could almost see their grief, coming from their stomachs, out of their mouths, swirling around the church and floating to the sky. He'd never seen his mom cry like that before, and hadn't since. He remembered the feeling of the tears slowly falling down his cheek, clouding his glasses, as one of his aunts patted him on the back.

Today, as always, it was still somber but a lot more peaceful. Mrs. Stone knelt down to the marker and rubbed it, while Suga closed her eyes in prayer.

Sometimes Daniel spoke out loud to it, sometimes he just stared at it, thinking.

"His soul is at rest," Suga said one time.

He thought about Avery Moore's soul, and her graveyard compared to his dad's.

While this one was newer, well manicured, Avery's felt forgotten. That grave deserved to be recognized. They could definitely do that with their project.

Daniel heard a sigh, pulling him out of his thoughts. Mrs. Stone got up and turned around, facing Daniel. She smiled a little.

"Okay. Are y'all ready?"

Daniel looked at his father's grave one more time.

He hoped Iris's dreams calmed down soon. He knew her well enough to know that if she wanted to explore again and find out about Avery Moore, she would, even if that meant going back to a haunted clearing. Or worse. He couldn't risk losing someone else close to him.

"Yes, Mama. Let's go."

CHAPTER
11

"I think that's Iris."

He opened the door and sure enough, his best friend walked into the house, carrying a notepad and a pen.

They were interviewing Suga for their project after school, and Daniel was admittedly a little nervous about it. He didn't know what Suga was going to do or if there were any superstitions of hers in place that would keep her from saying what she really wanted to say.

Still, he was determined. He knew that the sooner they found out about segregated graveyards, the sooner they could be done with this project, and Iris would stop having such bad dreams about graves and spirits.

"Hey, Daniel," Iris said, smiling and walking over to the couch. "Where's Suga?"

"She's upstairs. She'll be down in a second."

Daniel sat down beside Iris, his knee jumping up and down. His mom was at work, so there was no grown-up to buffer if things got weird.

"Relax," Iris said, grinning at him. Her eyes turned to the staircase.

"Hey, Suga!" she yelled.

"Well, heyyyy, babies!"

They heard her before they saw her. Pretty soon, Suga came downstairs in a pale pink housecoat, a matching bonnet, and slippers. She was holding a thin, worn brown book. She plopped in the armchair across from them.

"Now," she said, taking a deep breath. "What did you have to ask me?"

"Well," Daniel started, fidgeting with his glasses. "We're doing a project on segregation in Easaw, particularly graveyards and stuff. We—"

He started to say where he got the idea from, but decided against it.

"We knew we could ask you, especially from what you said in church on Sunday," Iris finished for him.

"Oh yes," Suga said. "Yes, times have changed. We've come so far, but still have a long way to go. Back when I was your age, everything was separated by Blacks only or

Whites only: sections in the library, bathrooms, restaurants, seats on the bus . . . When I was a teenager, though, people decided that they'd had enough. Just right here, in North Carolina, there were some protests at some of the restaurants in Greensboro. Some students went into a Whites-only lunch counter, demanding to be served. Customers pulled their hair, punched and spit on them . . . Oh, and the schools. Did you know that . . ." She stopped and sighed, staring off into space.

"What, Suga?" Iris pressed.

"Oh, child, it was awful. But you wanted to know about the cemeteries . . . A law passed when I was a child that made it legal to separate those who have passed on by race. When the caretakers of the Blacks-only cemeteries or sections of those cemeteries moved away, the graves were forgotten about, built on top of . . . sometimes even vandalized."

Iris gasped, and Daniel's stomach dropped.

"Some cemeteries would eventually have toppled headstones, vines everywhere . . ."

Iris and Daniel looked at each other.

"Where my Cecil is buried right now, Sampson's Perpetual Care, why, in my time period, he wouldn't even be able to be there. Oh, it was a tough time, babies. But forward we go, to make this world a better place." Suga smiled. "I'm so glad y'all are doing this. Such bright and helpful babies. You'll be rewarded, I'm sure."

Daniel's cheeks warmed while he saw Iris's tint the slightest pink. "Thanks, Suga."

"Well, look, I don't know if this helps, but I have some pictures of me as a little girl around Easaw. Maybe you can get a clearer picture of how things were around here."

She handed over the book, and Iris and Daniel scooted closer to get a look. They opened it up to find a little girl with tight curls, her mouth open in a wide smile, and a dripping ice cream cone in her hand.

"Is this you?" Daniel asked, pointing at the picture.

Suga leaned over the photo. "Oh yes! I used to love the ice cream parlor. Would use my allowance every week to get some. But do you see that diner, kinda in the background over there? Yes, we weren't allowed to eat there."

They turned the page, looking at Suga before she was Suga, when she was just a young Emma Mae, smiling, frowning, and in one, crying.

"I had just gotten my hair done and it hurt so bad!"

Suga said, laughing at the picture. "I'm sure you know that feeling." She winked at Iris.

"More than anything," Iris said, rolling her eyes at the thought of the tugging and pulling her hair dresser would do to give Iris her signature style.

The next picture was Suga standing on the porch of what looked like a small house in front of a pond. Iris peered closer. It looked like Nelson's Pond, the one behind her school.

"Oh, Suga, I forgot you lived around here before!" Iris said, smiling. Her eyes grew wide. "Hey, do you happen to know a Moore family? As a matter of fact, have you ever heard the name Avery Moore—"

The look Suga gave Iris was colder than all the snow in Easaw.

"What did you say?" Suga asked, her voice low.

Iris stammered. "A-Avery Moore. Did you know her?"

Daniel leaned forward to look at the picture, trying to focus their attention back on the photo album, but Suga snatched the book and closed it shut.

"Avery Moore was killed by the spirits of the snow."

Iris whipped her head toward Daniel, terror in her face. Daniel was bewildered.

What was Suga talking about?

"Suga?" Iris said, eyes wide. "What happened?"

"I'm going to my room," she said, taking the book. "I don't feel well. We can finish this later."

She walked upstairs.

Daniel groaned. Just when everything was going well, Suga had to do something weird, *again*. Iris's nightmares were going to be even worse now.

Iris watched Suga walk away, her mouth open in shock. "The spirits of the snow . . . actually killed somebody?" asked Iris quietly. She rubbed her arms. "So it's true. They're real."

"It's not true," Daniel grumbled. "It's just Suga being Suga. Let's get out of here."

Daniel was irritated that Suga brought up the spirits of the snow. But he couldn't help but wonder: What actually happened to Avery Moore?

CHAPTER 12

When they left Daniel's house, Iris's thoughts were spinning with the idea that the spirits of the snow really did kill Avery Moore.

Daniel, of course, didn't believe any of it, but at least now they both agreed that they wanted to find out exactly what *did* happen to her.

But it was hard. Suga clearly didn't want to say anything else about her. And once she'd decided something, there was no changing her mind.

They were reaching dead ends in their search for Avery. Moore was a very common last name in Easaw. Iris and Daniel reached out to the Moores they could find contact information for, but the ones who bothered to email them back had no idea who Avery was. Iris's dream was right: She *was* forgotten.

In the meantime, they had to focus on the center of their actual project: segregated graves. In social studies the next day, their teacher gave them free time at the end of class to discuss their projects. Some kids were chatting animatedly, like Heather, much to the annoyance of her partner, and Kayla, who was making great strides in her project about local sports teams with a kid named John. Kayla told Iris that they may be able to get some members of the local baseball team to come watch them present their project.

Iris and Daniel pushed their desks together and were reviewing the notes they had about the laws of segregated graveyards in the United States and North Carolina. Daniel had just found some information on how to get graveyards restored: through volunteer and nonprofit organizations. There were a few big ones in Easaw that Iris and Daniel had reached out to, but Iris also knew of one right under her nose.

"I have an idea," Iris said, putting her pencil down and looking at Daniel.

"What is it?" Daniel asked, his brow furrowed as he scribbled notes from his social studies book.

"So, you know how they were talking about helping people in church on Sunday?" Iris asked.

"Yeah."

"And all of the grown-ups are saying it's such a good idea that we're looking into the segregated graves around here? And how you just found that info about getting graves restored?"

"Yeah..."

"You know the school club, the Cleanup Club? They take a cause every few weeks and a volunteer group in town helps them complete it. We can join the club and ask if they'd want to help restore that graveyard in the clearing! It's perfect! We can get the student body and a volunteer group involved in one swoop."

It *was* perfect. Everyone would be talking about their project, and the graveyard would get cleaned up.

Daniel raised his eyebrows. "Wow, that is a good idea, Iris. When is their next meeting?"

"It's this afternoon, after school," a snooty voice said. "And we already *have* a cause."

Iris and Daniel looked up to find Heather smugly staring at them. Her partner, Sarah, who was in the middle of explaining something, closed her mouth and quietly turned to her book.

"This afternoon?" Iris's heart sank. She had step practice tonight.

"It's okay. I can go," Daniel whispered to her.

"We have an idea for a cause that the club might be interested in," Iris told Heather, leaning back and folding her arms.

"Didn't you hear me? We already *have* a cause. Chelsea, you know, my best friend? She's the president of that club. And we're fixing up the basketball court."

Daniel scrunched up his face. "There's nothing wrong with it."

"Yes, there is. It needs to be beautified!"

"Heather, it's a *basketball* court." Iris noticed Daniel's voice growing cold. "There are no cracks in the concrete, or anything. We have everything we need."

"It's an eyesore." Heather looked bored and turned back to Sarah. Iris rolled her eyes at Heather.

"I'm trying to understand who made Heather the queen of Nelson's Pond Middle," Iris said, a little louder than she should've. Kayla looked back at Iris and laughed, along with a few other kids, including Sarah. Daniel smiled and shook his head.

"Iris," Mr. Hammond said in warning, eyeing her over his glasses. How was he always able to hear her remarks and no one else's?

"Sorry," Iris mumbled quickly, then opened her mouth again. "Mr. Hammond, if someone wanted to start a service club, where we went around and cleaned up abandoned spaces in town, how would you recommend us going about it?"

"I'd say we already have a club that does that—the Cleanup Club."

You say we already have a club, but I can't even get my foot in the door, Iris was thinking, but instead she said:

"Well, Heather just informed me that the Cleanup Club already has a project going on, and I have an idea for a project that's very near and dear to my heart." Iris put her hands over her chest for good measure.

Mr. Hammond looked at Heather. "Now, Heather, did you say that? That's not true. We haven't voted on a project yet. I'm the advisor."

"Well, there's only one proposed project right now," Heather said sharply. When Mr. Hammond eyed her, she just smiled.

"Not anymore," Iris said.

"If you're interested, come to the meeting," said Mr. Hammond. "If the project is near and dear to your heart, we'd love to hear about it before we vote."

Mr. Hammond went back to grading test papers, and Iris went back to looking over notes for their project, making sure to stick her tongue out at Heather first.

CHAPTER 13

Although Mr. Hammond had encouraged Iris to go to the Cleanup Club meeting, she couldn't help but feel annoyed. She could've sworn she'd read in the school newspaper that they picked a day and time for the Cleanup Club that made it easy for any student to attend. She felt they assumed the step team girls would never want to participate, or that they were just forgotten about when the faculty checked on any clubs or teams that may overlap time wise. Plus, with Heather there and Chelsea as the president, they probably had everyone else pressured into voting for their project. How would Iris get enough votes to clean up the old cemetery? And fixing the perfectly good basketball court, of all things? That did nothing for anyone! At least cleaning up the cemetery would help people's loved ones get the respect and recognition they deserved. Iris's thoughts spiraled. She was cranky.

She hadn't had good sleep in days, waking up every few hours with a new nightmare, thinking that Avery was in her room.

"Iris!"

Iris jumped, making the remaining students in the classroom laugh.

"Yes, ma'am?"

"You're going to be late for your next class."

Sure enough, Iris looked around her English class and realized that, besides the few students who laughed at her while picking up their books and walking out of class, the room was empty. The first bell was still ringing.

"Oh—sorry, Mrs. Lawson. I was just thinking about something."

"Are you all right?" Mrs. Lawson looked at Iris with concern. Iris flashed her a smile.

"Yes. I was just daydreaming. Have a good day, Mrs. Lawson!" she added for good measure.

"You, too, Iris." She went back to gathering her own papers, and Iris sighed with relief.

Iris walked out of class into the busy hallway. All around her students were chatting, laughing, pretending to play basketball with balled-up pieces of paper. Iris blocked everything out, wandering through the hallway like she was a ghost herself.

"Iris!"

"Sorry, Mrs. Lawson! I—"

But Iris looked right into the eyes of Kayla.

"Mrs. Lawson? Girl, are you okay?"

Iris nodded a little too fast. *Act normal, Iris.*

"My bad, girl. I'm just thinking about a test. What's up?"

"I was asking are you ready for step practice after school?"

Kayla looked at Iris expectantly. Kayla was a slow learner when it came to stepping, but when she finally caught on and stepped with confidence, she was really good.

"Oh yeah. I have a new combination I want to try out today. I think it'll work really well."

Kayla nodded excitedly. "Okay, cool! And I could come to your house sometime to practice if I need to, right?"

"Of course, Kayla."

"Great. See you at practice!" Kayla whipped around, her fluffy curls bouncing behind her.

Iris walked through the crowd, clutching her books. She needed to focus. The dead couldn't take over her life.

"I'll see you after the meeting," Daniel said as they put their books back in their lockers. Daniel had agreed to check out the meeting and speak on behalf of their project.

"Okay. Let me know how it goes!"

"I will." Daniel walked away, his huge book bag taking over his skinny frame. Iris took a deep breath and exhaled, letting go of all her stresses of this school day.

Even though she was left out of the Young Captains ceremony and couldn't go to the Cleanup Club meeting, and girls like Heather tried to belittle step, she knew all that would be behind her once she got there.

It was time for step practice, one of Iris's favorite things in the world.

Because once she got there, all that would matter was the way her beads clanked against one another with every head turn, the way their stomps echoed through the gym, the precision of each straight arm, switching from left to right, the way they'd slap their thighs so many times in a row, they'd have red handprints on them when they got home. The way the team moved from spot to spot with each transition. The satisfaction of nailing the routine. She loved step. And no one, not Heather or even Avery, was going to take that away from her.

Iris went into the bathroom and changed into sneakers, sweatpants, and her blue-and-yellow step team shirt, and pulled her braids back into a beaded ponytail. She looked around for other girls to walk to practice with but didn't see any of them. Maybe it was for the better. As the captain, she liked to be the first one to arrive.

She waited for the other girls to show up, going over one of their most complicated steps in her head.

"Hey!"

Iris almost jumped out of her skin.

She turned around to see Naomi, one of the other girls on the step team. Naomi was really good, one of the best. When Iris wasn't leading the more popular steps, she called on Naomi to do it.

"You okay?" Naomi said, peering at Iris. "You look sick."

"Hey, girl," Iris said. "Yeah, I'm fine. I'm just . . . cold."

The word was thick on her tongue.

"Oh. Well, we'll warm up soon enough, right?" Naomi said, getting on the floor to stretch.

"Yup. That's right."

Pretty soon, the other girls showed up, dressed out and ready for practice. Iris sighed, letting go of her uneasiness.

"I have a new combination I'm working on for us," Iris said, pacing in front of the girls. Their advisor was sitting in the back of the gym, half watching, half working on paperwork. She was nice enough, but quiet, and didn't really know a lot about the step team. "Let's start off with the Dazed step, and afterward, go into the No One Can Step Like Us transition. I think those flow *really* well together. Naomi's going to start off Dazed, and I'm going to lead the transition step."

The girls murmured, saying this new arrangement sounded like a good idea.

Iris smiled.

"Okay. Let's do it," she said, lining up behind Naomi.

"Naomi? On your count."

Naomi cleared her throat. "Five . . . six . . . seven . . . eight!"

Stomp . . . stomp . . . clap . . . stomp . . . clap . . .

Naomi started the step off slowly, her arms windmilling with each move.

Left . . . right . . . left . . . right . . .

Her head turned from side to side, every movement as slow as molasses.

Then she stopped. She stood in place.

"Dazed!" she called out.

From there, all the girls joined in, doing exactly what Naomi did, but faster, all the stomps, claps, and arm and head motions coming together to make one cohesive beat. Iris named this step *Dazed* because that's how she felt when she was done doing it: dizzy from the head swinging and dazed from the crowd cheering her on.

The step ended, and the girls stood in place, their arms tight by their sides. They were about to transition into a new formation, and it was Iris's turned to lead.

"There's no use of cry*ing*, no reason to *fuss*!" Iris chanted, doing a step for each syllable.

"*No* other step team can step like *us*!

"We *came*, to step, and that's what we'll *do*!

"We are the Nelson's Pond girls wearing *yel*low and *blue*!"

The other girls repeated the chant, joining in the step, but this time they moved to a new transition—instead of four straight lines, they became a diamond, where Iris would be the tip.

"Kayla! Straighten out that arm!" Iris called out.

They did this chant four times until the diamond shape was formed. When they all took the final step together, it boomed, echoing through the gym.

Silence, then—

"Iris! That was amazing. That goes together *way* better than the other transition!" Jeanie, another girl on the step team, said.

"Thanks," Iris said, smiling.

"You're so good at this. You're so creative! How do you make up these steps?"

"I come up with the beat first," Iris explained. "What I want it to sound like . . . then I make up the movements to go with it."

"You have a real talent for this, Iris!" Jeanie said. "You're such a great captain."

The other girls nodded and patted Iris on the back, and despite herself, Iris felt good. Of course she still felt bad about not being invited to the Young Captains Award Ceremony, but her teammates recognized her, and that still meant something.

"We're all talented," she said.

Kayla looked down and shuffled her feet.

"*All* of us," Iris repeated. "We all have different strengths. I couldn't have a team by myself."

The girls continued step practice, laughing, stepping, helping one another.

When practice ended, Iris felt lighter and warmer than she had in a while. She went over to discuss some things with her advisor while the other girls headed to the locker room.

By the time Iris finished and walked outside, all the other girls had already been picked up or had headed home. Iris was alone again.

A gust of wind blew hard, making her stumble, almost as though someone had pushed her from behind. Iris shivered in the cold air. The feeling of dread crept back in.

Iris and Daniel had agreed to meet up after Iris's practice and walk home together, so she could hear about the meeting immediately. The more Daniel talked about the Cleanup Club meeting, the angrier Iris got.

"I gave them some facts about the segregated cemetery situation in North Carolina and Easaw, and told them that we believed we found one within walking distance to the school," Daniel said as they walked across campus. "Heather was trying to challenge me with everything I said—even when Chelsea was trying to be receptive. She kept talking about how she's already talked to volunteers about fixing up the basketball court, and how excited they already were . . . to me, it sounds like she's pushing for it to be less about fixing up the court, and more about planting flowers, which makes no sense really, because it's all concrete! Planting flowers is fine, but planting flowers around the outskirts of a basketball court for this purpose seems like a waste of people's time to me. Then, she took a dig at the court itself, saying that if she had her way, she'd just do away with it altogether."

Iris stopped in her tracks, noting the edge in Daniel's voice. "She said *what*?"

Daniel nodded. "I don't think it's a lost cause, though. I think Heather is threatened by the idea that her project might not get voted on, because she only tried to talk down on the cemetery cleanup anytime someone else had something good to say about it. Even Mr. Hammond said that the historical context of it was really intriguing. He said he can't wait to see our project."

The historical context . . .

If Mr. Hammond was intrigued by that part, they needed more historical context. He was the advisor— maybe he could sway the decision. It wasn't just about her beating Heather. It was about Avery, and all the other people laid to rest there.

And about having the best project.

Iris grabbed Daniel's arm. "Come on," she said. "Let's go back to the library."

"Now?"

"Yes, just for a little while! We have some more research to do on the project."

They turned back around in the direction of the school, a strong gust of wind guiding them there.

Iris and Daniel walked to the nonfiction section of the school library.

"If Mr. Hammond was moved by the historical context of the cemetery, then let's give it to him," Iris said, marching through the library, Daniel by her side. They needed something else to drive their point home and make this project the best it could be. It needed to be voted on.

"Suga said even the town library was segregated before," Daniel said, running his hands down the spines of the worn, older books.

Iris paused, her eyes suddenly wide. "This *school* was probably segregated at one point! When did it open?"

Maybe reminding students that their own school had been segregated would make them care about the people still segregated in their graves.

"I can't remember, but we can easily find out," Daniel said, stopping at one book and pulling it straight out: *The History of Nelson's Pond Middle.* It was a thin book. Iris noticed it was published by The Old North Publishing, a local publishing company. She remembered the name because another student was doing their project about it. "Look!" Daniel continued. "We can find out when this school opened, and if segregation was still legal here back then."

"Good idea," Iris said. The two of them sat down and flipped through pages, skimming past lots of blurry black-and-white images of Nelson's Pond on the wooded land before the school was built. She thought of the photo of Suga, posing in front of her house near the pond. She didn't recall Suga ever saying she attended Nelson's Pond Middle. Maybe it really *was* segregated back then.

With each page flip, there was more history about Nelson's Pond. Iris was getting impatient. The historical context of the pond had nothing to do with the cemetery she wanted the Cleanup Club to restore.

They turned the page again.

Iris saw five White men in suits, holding shovels and wearing hard hats. According to the caption, one of them was named George Nelson.

"This is when they broke ground for the school," Iris whispered, turning another page.

Next there was a picture of the first class of students to graduate from Nelson's Pond Middle, in 1950.

"I guess the school *wasn't* integrated at this point," Daniel said, looking over the smiling White faces and turning the page.

"Wait," Iris said, grabbing his arm. "Look!"

There was a small section on the bottom left-hand page, talking about the desegregation of Nelson's Pond Middle in 1955.

Daniel ran his fingers over the small, grainy picture.

There were nine Black children sitting in chairs, some smiling, some solemn, all clutching their books.

Iris suddenly felt sad, thinking about what they must've gone through trying to fit in. How they probably wanted to cry, or be upset, but had to keep going, learning.

She looked closer, her eyes scanning the bottom of the page. Wanting to know more.

Then she screamed and jumped back out of her seat, ignoring the librarian's plea to be quiet as she looked at the face, frozen in time, the same face that visited her in her dreams. There, in the photo, was a young girl with two pigtails and round eyes. Only here, they were sparkling, not those dark eye sockets that seemed to suck the light from a room.

"What? What's wrong?" Daniel asked.

She pointed at the fourth name.

Avery Moore.

CHAPTER 14

This was no dream, no nightmare. Avery Moore's spirit was really visiting her.

"Daniel!" she exclaimed, the librarian shushing her again. "This is the exact face I've been dreaming about! I had never seen—never even *heard* of Avery Moore until we saw that grave! How could I be dreaming about her? I think—I think she's really visiting me!"

Iris was shaking. There was an actual ghost coming into her room at night. No wonder her dreams felt different than all the other ones. They *weren't* dreams.

Daniel had a funny look on his face as he stared at Iris.

"Iris," Daniel said cautiously. "You had to have seen her somewhere before, maybe in one of our history books. You know, I read that you can't dream of a face you've never seen, it's always a face you've seen before, even if it was a stranger's that you've only seen one time . . ."

"It's *not* a dream, Daniel," Iris said, slightly irritated. Wasn't he listening? "She's actually visiting me. That explains why there was a smudge on that picture I took. That was *her*. Why my room always feels so cold when I see her. Why my windows are always open the next morning. She's real and . . . and . . ."

She trailed off, her mind spinning. Why was the ghost of Avery Moore visiting Iris? What did she want?

"Iris Rose, I only want to be your friend," the spirit said. *"Remember me."*

Remember her.

Avery Moore was one of the first students to desegregate Nelson's Pond Middle.

Why hadn't she heard about her before? In the history books, like Daniel said? She would've remembered that.

A girl who did a great thing, who was maybe killed by the spirits of the snow, was buried in an abandoned, segregated graveyard in her neighborhood? Why wasn't there anything in the school, on the Hall of Fame wall, talking about Avery or the other eight kids?

This was happening for a reason. She'd never seen Avery before, but now both images of her, alive and dead, were stained in her mind.

If there was no trace of Avery even going to this school when she was one of the nine who desegregated it, the same thing was on track to happen to Iris, her step team, her project. She wouldn't let that happen.

She wouldn't let this project go to the wayside. She wouldn't let the people in this school forget anyone else.

Avery wanted to be remembered, just like Iris. They'd remember Avery with their project, and she'd probably go away.

Right?

Iris looked up to find Daniel staring at her for a long while, a sad expression on his face.

"What?" Iris asked. She knew Daniel probably didn't believe her. This was hard to believe herself.

He just shook his head. "Nothing. This information about Avery desegregating the school is just the historical context our project needs." He scribbled down notes. "She deserves a better grave."

Iris and Daniel worked as long as they could before the librarian kicked them out. Daniel was upset, too, especially when he thought about his own father. "Someone's dad is buried in that graveyard," Daniel had said as they looked through the archives of old newspapers in the library. "Can you imagine? Not knowing where your dad was buried?"

In most articles, the students who desegregated Nelson's Pond Middle weren't mentioned by name. They were referred to as "colored" or "the Nelson Nine." Once Iris and Daniel found that out, they were able to uncover more information about the nine kids who desegregated the school, even if they were only mentioned as a group.

They dove deeper and deeper into the desegregation of Nelson's Pond Middle. With every article, Iris realized that the decision wasn't met with open arms.

There were protests: adults showing up to the Nelson Nine's first day of school with signs saying things like WHITES ONLY and KEEP THIS SCHOOL CLEAN. Avery and the others were spit on, their hair was pulled, and things were thrown at them, when all they wanted to do was go to school. To learn.

Iris walked home, lost in thought. The ghost of a girl who desegregated Iris's own middle school was visiting her at night, asking to be her friend, asking to be remembered.

No wonder nobody cared about her step team. Some of the protesters' children may have taught at Nelson's Pond Middle; their grandchildren probably were sitting right beside Iris every day.

She walked back home, opened the door, and was bombarded by a loudly screaming Vashti.

"Iris! I have a great idea," she said, grinning and jumping up and down. She wore a pink, frilly nightgown with a brown Barbie doll on the front. She waved an identical doll around in her hands. "We can play step team with *dolls*! We can put on a show in front of their dollhouse. Your doll can be the captain, and mine—"

"Not now, 'Ti," said Iris, trying to climb up the stairs.

Vashti's lower lip trembled. "But—"

"Babygirl! The food is almost ready." Mr. Rose came into the foyer with a big grin on his face. He whispered to the girls, "Don't tell your mother, but I got some fruit punch soda for us."

Vashti squealed, looking bright eyed at Iris. It was a not-so-secret secret that Mrs. Rose hated soda, and Mr. Rose loved it.

Iris smiled weakly, but Daddy was onto her.

"What's wrong?"

Iris couldn't even answer this question. What *was* wrong? Fruit punch soda and dolls and step shows were all the things that made a perfect night. Why didn't she feel it?

She was sleepy, but too afraid to sleep. She was sad and mad and . . . scared.

"I think I'm just tired," she said, forcing a yawn, watching her mom walk to the foyer where the rest of her family was standing. "Can I eat upstairs?"

Mrs. Rose looked at Mr. Rose with raised eyebrows. "Iris isn't feeling well," he said, answering her silent question. He turned to Iris. "You can eat upstairs tonight, but you know the rules. No red drinks upstairs. You'll have to drink something else." Iris couldn't tell if it was disappointment or concern in his face.

"Iris . . . are you really eating upstairs?" Vashti pouted.

Iris hesitated. She could have fruit punch soda if she ate down here. And the season finale of her favorite show came on tonight.

"Okay, I'll stay."

Vashti squealed, and the four of them walked to the dining room, where a warm, filling dinner of chili and cornbread was laid out. Iris's stomach growled.

"Vashti, do you want to say grace tonight?" Mama asked.

Vashti nodded, cleared her throat, squeezed her eyes shut, and said a singsongy prayer. She forgot some of it in the middle and giggled. Iris rolled her eyes.

"Amen! Let's eat," Daddy said.

And they ate, Iris getting sleepier and sleepier by the minute, eating pretty much in silence. She thought about telling her parents about Avery. Maybe it would ease her thoughts.

"Mama," Iris said, swallowing her food. "Daddy. Um . . . Daniel and I found some interesting information about our project."

"Oh?" Daddy said, helping himself to another serving of chili. "What's that?"

"Well, remember when I told you about that gravestone we saw? Avery Moore?"

"Yes," Mama said, giving Iris a knowing look. "You haven't been back there, have you?"

"No, Mama," Iris said, fighting the edge in her voice, eager to get to the point. "We found out some more information about her. She was actually one of the first students to integrate Nelson's Pond."

"Really?" her parents said in unison. "How did you find that out?" Mama asked.

"In the library," Iris said. "But it's strange, because neither she nor any of the other students are on the Hall of Fame wall at school. We only found them in one book."

"It seems like you're going to be the one doing the teaching when you present your project," Daddy said. "That's quite a piece of information."

"Yeah," Iris said, piping up. "I can't wait to show Heather and all of the other girls that my project *deserves* to be talked about."

"Iris," Mama said sternly. "Remember what I told you about that. You don't need to prove anything to anyone. Just do it for you."

"Yeah, that's what I meant," Iris said quickly. "But they need to *see*—"

"Chasing the approval of these girls will leave you disappointed. Some people will never change, no matter what you show them," Mama said. "It'll drive you up the wall. Focus on doing your best."

Deep down, Iris knew Mama was right. "Yes, ma'am," she said.

Mama smiled. "But that is a great piece of information. Go, Iris."

Iris's heart swelled. Her parents were finally paying attention to her the way they used to.

"We're trying to submit the project to the Cleanup Club, so we can get together and clean the graveyard. Daniel went to the meeting this afternoon, but he said some of the girls today were dead set on some other stupid project."

"Really?" Mama sighed. "I hate how cliquey these things can be."

"Yeah. He said that they pretty much brushed him off, and ragged on the basketball court and want to spruce it up."

"Well, they've got some nerve. Do your best on your project, Iris, and we'll cross that bridge if we need to." Iris could practically see her mama dialing the principal's number in her mind.

"Mama, can I watch TV now?" Vashti interrupted.

"It's my TV night, 'Ti," Iris said.

"Iris, what are you thinking about watching?" Mama asked.

"The season finale of *Missy Mysteries* is coming on," Iris said.

"You know, some of the guys at work were saying they watched that with their daughters and it was pretty good," Daddy said. "I'll go set it up."

Even though she was still full, Iris popped a bag of popcorn and put it in a big purple bowl. She squeezed in between her dad and Vashti, whose hand instantly reached in her popcorn bowl.

"Can I have some first," she muttered. Vashti smiled as she threw the handful in her mouth.

"All right, here we go." Daddy hit the play button while Mama turned off the lights and sat beside him.

Iris relaxed and lay back, grabbing a fistful of popcorn herself.

They weren't even ten minutes into the show before Vashti started crying.

"It's too scary!" she whined, covering her eyes and almost knocking the popcorn out of Iris's hand.

"Vashti, be quiet. It's not real."

The green monster on the screen that Missy was fighting wasn't nearly as creepy as Avery. Iris shuddered and instinctively looked behind her to the dark staircase leading up to her room.

When Vashti started sniffling, though, her Dad paused the show.

"Vashti?"

"It's too scary, Daddy!" she cried. Fat tears ran down her cheeks. "Can we turn it off?"

Daddy gave Iris a look.

"No, Daddy!" Iris yelled. "Can't she go upstairs or something until it's over?"

Vashti screamed. "No! I can't go up there by myself now! *She's* up there!"

"Now, Vashti, sweetie, there's no one upstairs," her mom said, leaning over to look at her.

She?

No. Vashti was just being a baby.

Their Dad looked at Iris. "Iris, maybe we can finish watching this after Vashti goes to sleep."

"It'll be about Iris's bedtime then," Mama said. "Sweetie, can't we watch it tomorrow night?"

Iris wanted to scream. Everyone was going to be talking about this at school tomorrow. After the day she had, all she wanted to do was watch her show. She had to give that up, too? All because Vashti was being a baby?

"Do you want to try to find something else?" her mom asked.

What else could she watch with Vashti crying in her ear? A baby cartoon?

"No thanks, Mama," she said. "I think I'm going to just go to bed early."

She got off the couch, dropped the empty popcorn bowl in the dishwasher, and wandered upstairs.

Vashti was still throwing a tantrum, crying about being scared. She ran in front of Iris and blocked the stairway.

"'Ti, come on," Iris mumbled.

"You can't go up there, Sissy! *She's* up there!" Vashti yelled, tears streaming down her face.

"Vashti, move and stop being ridiculous," Iris snapped. She didn't have time to think about Vashti and her dolls.

Vashti was holding firm, not letting go of the stair rail even when Iris tried to pick her up. *"Nooo!"*

"Vashti, *move!"*

Vashti let go at the exact same moment that Iris gave another tug, sending both girls tumbling toward the ground. Vashti hit her head on the bottom stair and started wailing.

"What are y'all doing in here?"

Mrs. Rose ran into the foyer to see Vashti crying and Iris huffing as she helped her sister to her feet.

"Vashti wouldn't move and I'm trying to go upstairs."

"She can't go up there!"

"'Ti, will you please cut the dramatics? Gosh, you act like such a big baby."

"Hey!" Mrs. Rose yelled, pointing at Iris. "There will be none of that."

Iris looked up at her mother, exasperated. "Me? So you're not going to acknowledge that Vashti was trying to block me from going to my own room?"

"Iris, she's four. And she hit her head. Vashti, go in the kitchen with your dad so he can see if you need ice for your forehead."

Vashti wandered away from the foyer, still whimpering, rubbing her head.

"Iris Rose, what has gotten into you?"

"Mama, I didn't do anything."

"You're yelling at your sister! She's sensitive, Iris. And she misses you. You've barely paid any attention to her lately."

Iris sucked her teeth. "Oh, so I'm the bad guy all around now."

Mrs. Rose narrowed her eyes. "I know you didn't just suck your teeth at me. And watch your tone. What's all that talk about?"

"Nothing," Iris mumbled. "I'm sorry."

Mrs. Rose looked Iris in her eyes, her sternness melting away into concern. "Iris, are you sure you're okay? You can talk to me, you know. About anything."

Iris debated talking to her mom about her strange day. Would her mother believe her if she said she thought *something*—something like a ghost—had been visiting her?

"Mama?" she looked up at her mama's brown eyes and watched them soften.

"Yes, baby?"

"Do you—do you believe in ghosts?"

"Oh, sweetheart. I think the research about graves and Suga's superstitions are starting to get to you."

"Mama, I've been dreaming about the girl on one of the graves I've seen—Avery Moore." Iris tried again. "But, I'd never seen her face in a photo before today. But it was the same face . . . that I dreamed about . . ."

Her mom's brows knit together. "You're having more nightmares? You can keep your night-light plugged in." Mama lowered her voice. "I won't tell anyone."

"No, Mama." Iris was getting desperate. "I don't think they're dreams. My room becomes cold. My window is open when I wake up. It's real . . ." Iris trailed off. She knew she wasn't making any sense. Her mom was nodding her head, trying to understand, but Iris could tell she didn't.

"It sounds like you're sleepwalking, baby," she said, taking her daughter and hugging her. "I can't even believe I'm suggesting this, but maybe you should focus on your project earlier in the day, so it won't bleed into your dreams."

Sleepwalking? Iris hadn't even considered that. But maybe . . . maybe she *was* sleepwalking, opening her window, and that's why she would feel so cold at night.

But how did she dream of Avery's face? Maybe she really did see it before, like Daniel said.

Iris didn't know what to believe.

"I know it's hard, baby, with your project and the step team, but you'll be okay."

Iris relaxed a little until she heard her sister whimper, her dad's cool voice soothing her.

"You're okay?" Mama said, glancing toward the kitchen. Iris could tell Mama was distracted by Vashti now.

Iris just nodded, feeling down again.

"Are you sure?"

"Yes, Mama. I-I promise."

"Okay." Mrs. Rose furrowed her brow. Iris wasn't sure that her mother believed her. "Come apologize to your sister."

Iris walked with her mother to the kitchen, where her sister was sniffling. Vashti cut her eyes at Iris.

Mrs. Rose looked at her head. "There's no knot, thank goodness. I think you'll be okay, baby."

Daddy looked at Iris pointedly.

Iris sighed. "'Ti . . . I'm sorry for pulling you down. And not playing with you lately. But guess what! You know I'm out of school next week for winter break. We'll have plenty of time to play then."

Vashti's angry, wet face opened up into a grin. "You promise?"

Iris hesitated. "Yes. I promise. We'll have plenty of time to play together."

"See, Vashti? You just have to be patient, okay?" Dad told her sister.

"I'm going to go upstairs and get ready for bed early," Iris announced, wishing she would've just done that instead of foolishly thinking she'd enjoy a TV show.

She said goodnight to Daddy and Vashti, raced upstairs, and let her mom wrap her hair, kissing her goodnight.

She was tired, but when the house fell silent, she was nervous.

She could be sleepwalking, that was the most logical explanation...

But what if she wasn't?

Avery could be making her way to her window. Right now.

She fought against her heavy eyelids, trying to stay up, watching the shadows the night-light cast in her room. Even if she was just sleepwalking, she didn't want to have another nightmare about Avery. She thought of Avery's face in that picture. Thought of Avery's ghost, haunting her. For once, she wished her parents let her drink coffee.

Tap-tap-tap.

She heard it again. That tap on her window.

She trained her eyes on the night-light.

Don't be afraid, she told herself. *You haven't been asleep yet, so you aren't sleepwalking. Just look up, and prove to yourself that it's just a branch rubbing against the window.*

Iris pinched herself, the sting assuring her she was wide-awake.

Tap-tap-tap.

One the count of three, Iris thought. *One … two … three …*

She glanced up.

A girl was staring in her direction. Her eyes swallowed the night sky.

Avery.

The night-light flickered, then went out, leaving Iris in total darkness.

CHAPTER 15

A scream left Iris's mouth, but it disappeared into the thick darkness before it could make a sound.

"I don't want to hurt you," Avery whispered. "I need your help."

Iris wasn't frozen to her bed. She wasn't sleepwalking. This was real.

She slid off her bed, knocking her knee on her nightstand, and stumbled backward onto the floor. Shivering, she slowly inched backward to the door.

But before she could run to her parents' room, she stopped. Escaping now meant nothing if Avery would just keep coming back. She needed to face this. To stop this.

"Please, just leave me alone," Iris whispered, her eyes filling with tears.

"Help me be remembered. I don't know who I am anymore." Iris could hear Avery more than she could see her.

She struggled to get enough breath to speak. "You're Avery Moore," Iris said. "One of the first nine Black students to attend Nelson's Pond Middle. It was a historical moment . . . a great thing . . ." Iris felt as if she were reading the history book she saw today.

She looked up at Avery's shimmering figure, her black eyes staring at Iris.

"Maybe you were killed by a spirit of the snow."

"I've never heard of such spirits."

Iris took a deep, shuddering breath. Inhale, exhale the fear.

"Please. That's all I know."

"I did a great thing, you say? Why have I been forgotten in death?" Avery's voice went from high-pitched to something deeper, more sinister, and it frightened Iris. What if she lashed out at her?

Tears falling from Iris's eyes blurred the ghost in front of her.

"Look, I feel forgotten, too, a lot of the time," Iris said quickly. "My mom said if my school doesn't want to recognize me, then it's their loss."

"Oh, but they will. They will see, Iris Rose, and you will make them."

Iris started at the edge in Avery's voice. Her voice grew deeper, even deeper than Daddy's in a split second.

What did she mean by that?

"You can change things for the both of us, and show those who have doubted us," Avery said, seemingly reading Iris's thoughts. "Once and for all, they'll see. They'll remember me. We will stop at nothing to make them."

Iris thought about her mom's words from earlier.

They didn't match up with Avery's.

Iris lay there, letting Avery's words cover her.

"I have a way. Come with me."

Iris thought of everything with the Cleanup Club, the Young Captains Society, with Vashti, with her project, with her step team. She didn't want to be forgotten ever again.

The moon hid behind a cloud, making her room a little darker.

Avery held out her hand, and a sharp, cool wind hit Iris in her face.

Somewhere in the back of her mind, she thought of how Daniel would tell her how dangerous this was.

But Iris took the hand of the ghost.

With a touch so cold it pained Iris, blinded her, and with a swirl of snow and sadness and anger, Iris went where Avery took her. She had the sensation of falling in a dream, but she knew she was very much awake.

And when she opened her eyes, she saw nothing.

CHAPTER 16

Iris whirled around, her eyes adjusting to the darkness. There were trees. Faint, blinking Christmas lights in the distance. Snow under her feet.

She was in the clearing.

Avery materialized in front of her. She glided toward Iris, her arms outstretched to the graves surrounding them.

"You're just like us. These people were forgotten," Avery said. "We ALL have been forgotten."

Iris said nothing, only nodded.

"If you are my forever friend, we will never be forgotten again," Avery said, Iris getting colder the closer she got. "You'll see."

Avery wasn't a spirit of the snow, or a nightmare. She was a girl who wanted to be remembered, just like Iris.

"I only want to be your friend," Avery repeated, her black eyes absorbing the moonlight. "What do you say?"

Iris hesitated, almost hearing Daniel's plea to leave this ghost alone, her mom's words about not seeking recognition.

She shook her head to rid her mind of those thoughts, and nodded.

Avery grinned, one that was too wide, too slow. It took up her face. Iris thought it would go past her ears.

"Let's play," Avery said, her voice high-pitched again.

Avery held her hands over the ground, and a gust of wind formed, rolling the powder into a ball. She sent the ball flying toward Iris, and the cold stung a bit, soaking through her pajamas to her skin.

A snowball fight.

Avery giggled, a too-fast titter.

Iris scooped a handful of snow off the ground, her fingers scraping the grave underneath. It felt wrong to play out here knowing who was beneath her feet.

Avery threw another snowball, hitting Iris squarely in her chest. "It just came back to me . . . There are few things I loved more than playing in the snow."

Iris smiled and molded the snow in her hands and hurled it at Avery. Avery squealed as the ball went through her chest to the ground behind her. Her squeal echoed off the trees, lingering a little longer than it should have.

But Iris kept playing, kept gathering snow and hurling it through the air. The exertion took her mind off everything that had happened earlier. The longer she played, the more she felt like she was dreaming, removed from the real world. The edges of her vision were getting fuzzy. She felt numb. She no longer felt her hands as she gathered up the snowballs. It seemed as if time was moving slower. It was taking her longer to gather up snow to make the snowballs, especially since she couldn't feel her fingers.

After a while, she grew tired. Iris realized that she was warm enough from running around that it would probably be okay if she lay down for a little bit. She curled up on top of the graves to rest. The powdery snow was soft, comfortable, and Iris burrowed deeper into it. Avery hovered over her, humming a little song.

Suddenly, there was a bright light behind Avery, illuminating every part of her except her eyes.

"Hey. What's going on?" Iris asked. She peered behind Avery and squinted her eyes.

It was her neighbors with the Christmas lights. They had turned on their back porch light.

Avery was still as a statue.

"Is someone back there?" Iris heard someone call faintly.

Oh no. If Iris was caught back here, she'd be in so much trouble.

She inched backward, deeper into the woods.

"Avery," Iris whispered. "Help me hide."

But Avery was gone.

Iris whipped around, only greeted by the pitch-black darkness of the woods behind her.

She heard the voice say, "No one there," and the porch light turned back off, leaving the colorful lights in its wake.

She shivered violently, feeling all the melted snow on her bare skin.

"Avery?"

Iris heard nothing. The trees moved silently above her head.

The ice around Avery's grave sparkled in the night sky.

She was alone, in a graveyard, covered in snow.

She had to get out of here. Fast.

As quietly as she could, she ran past the neighbors' house, praying that they were already back in bed, not looking for anyone anymore. She kept running, across the street, and ended up at her front door. She didn't have her key, so she had to knock.

What was she going to say when her parents saw her out here?

She couldn't think about it.

She knocked on the door again, frantic.

"Who could that be, this late?" she heard Daddy ask Mama as their footsteps got closer and closer to the door.

Daddy opened the door. Her mom was standing in the foyer, her eyes wide.

"Mama," Iris said, wrapping her arms around her mom, shivering. She was starting to feel exactly how afraid she was, relieved she was. She was so glad to be home.

"Iris!" Mrs. Rose's eyes flitted from anger, to concern, to fear. "What are you doing outside? With no jacket? How did you . . . ?"

Get out there? Iris wanted to finish her mother's sentence. *A ghost took me.*

Iris opened her mouth to speak, but her throat tensed, her nose burned, her arms tingled as she started crying. "I was sleeping and the next thing I knew, I was outside!" Iris was bawling. She heard Vashti run downstairs. "I didn't sneak outside, Mama, I promise!"

"Iris!" Daddy knelt down in front of his daughter. "Are you hurt? Did you see someone out there?" He looked behind Iris, narrowing his eyes at whatever he thought was lurking.

Iris shook her head, crying, her nose and face wet. "I'm not hurt," she sniffled.

"It's okay, baby, we've got you," Mama said as her parents pulled Iris tighter. Iris hugged them back—relieved, but unable to ignore the pain as the feeling came back to her fingers. It pushed more tears out of her eyes, but she knew her parents just thought she was afraid. "Iris, you're soaked! Baby . . . you've been sleepwalking again."

"Huh?"

Mr. and Mrs. Rose looked at each other and nodded.

"You sleepwalked straight outside! We didn't hear you slip out." Mrs. Rose put her hand in her hair and sighed.

Iris could see her mom's mind working, looking for an answer. "Your sleeping habits have been so fitful lately. Vashti's, too. Were you on your tablet?"

Iris just nodded, then sank into her mother's arms, the adrenaline running out of her body.

"Well, no more tablet time after dinner."

Iris looked up. "Mama! You're punishing me after what just happened?"

"I'm not punishing you, Iris! But you're sleepwalking! Every time you fall asleep on that tablet, your sleeping patterns change," she said. "This is dangerous! Anything could've happened to you out there! How far did you get?"

Iris didn't want to tell her about the clearing. She felt it would make her parents even more nervous than they already were.

"I only got to the mailbox," she said. *Another lie.*

Mrs. Rose looked at Mr. Rose and threw her hands in the air. "Imagine if she would've tried to cross the street! Sleepwalking!"

"This weekend, I'll install bolt locks on the front and back doors," Mr. Rose declared, giving Iris a kiss on her forehead. "It'll be okay."

Vashti tugged on Iris's pant leg, her sleepy face scrunched up in a confused expression. "Sissy," she said. "Sissy—"

"Sissy is going to bed now, Vashti." Mama turned back to Iris. "I'm taking you upstairs and getting you out of these clothes. And I'm taking the tablet. Come on." Mrs. Rose led Iris upstairs.

"No! Sissy! Wait!" Vashti screeched, running upstairs behind the two of them.

"Hey!" shouted Mr. Rose. "Vashti, you heard your mother. You'll have to talk to Sissy in the morning. She's not feeling well tonight. Let's go back to bed."

Vashti's screams and cries followed Iris and Mrs. Rose all the way up to Iris's room. "I have to tell her!" she heard her little sister cry faintly.

Mrs. Rose sighed. "Vashti's been so upset all night. She must've known something was going on with her sister."

"Yeah," was all Iris could say. She felt weak.

They walked upstairs. Mrs. Rose looked through Iris's drawers and picked out the warmest pajamas she could find and gave them to Iris. She had to admit that Avery's plan worked. She was getting all the attention again.

"Iris, honey, is there anything else going on?"

Iris froze and looked up at her mother. "What do you mean?"

"Is there something else going on that you want to talk about? Something that's been bothering you?" Mrs. Rose looked at her daughter intently. "I know things are hard with your baby sister right now, and being left out of the Young Captains ceremony, and you are working so hard on your project and your Cleanup Club . . . but it'll get better. Vashti just wants to be like you, and if your school decides not to notice you, that's their loss. You'll continue to do great things while they get left behind."

"No, Mama. I'm okay."

"Okay, baby. Well, give me your tablet."

Iris sighed as she handed over her tablet to her mother.

"I'll give it back to you in the morning. I love you."

"I love you, too."

"Do you want me to keep the night-light on?" Mrs. Rose tried to ask as casually as possible. It must've flickered back on in Avery's absence.

Iris sighed again. "Yes, please."

After Iris's mom closed the door, Iris lay there, replaying the night. The idea of her being out there, in the dark, alone, made her shiver all over again. Avery said she wanted a friend. A forever friend. She couldn't wait to discuss this with Daniel, knowing what he might say. Iris was still shivering. It felt like a million little needles were sticking her in her fingers as the feeling came back to them.

Any chance of Iris falling asleep escaped the night.

Was Avery trying to be Iris's friend?

Or trying to hurt her?

CHAPTER 17

Iris was so drowsy the next morning she felt like she might faint. It seemed as if she'd only blinked before her mother shook her awake.

"Are you okay?" Mama asked. "Do you need the day off from school? You had a long night."

Iris considered this, but she had step practice after school, and she needed to tell Daniel what happened as soon as she could. And she needed to work on her project. She still wanted to help Avery get the recognition she deserved. Even if Avery already had a plan of her own.

"I'm okay, Mama," she finally said, before taking a long, hot shower, getting dressed, and meeting Daniel outside.

When he saw her, he opened his mouth to say hello, but his face quickly turned to concern when he saw Iris. She could only imagine how tired she looked.

"What's wrong?" he asked when she approached him.

"Daniel, I need you to listen to me."

"What is it?"

"Last night, after I went up to my room, Avery came again," she said, lowering her voice. "I went with her to the clearing."

As Iris recapped last night, she noticed Daniel's face turning a sickly shade of green.

"My mom thinks I was sleepwalking, and Daddy said he'd put up bolt locks to keep me from leaving. But it was *Avery* that took me out there, Daniel—"

"Iris, this has got to stop." Daniel used a tone Iris had never heard before. "You could've frozen to death! We need to finish this project so you can stop sleepwalking. I'm glad your dad is putting up bolt locks."

They stopped on the sidewalk on the way to school, and Iris looked at Daniel. "Daniel, are you even hearing me?" Iris said. "It doesn't matter if he puts bolt locks on the doors because I didn't *leave* through the door. I went through the window, because that's how Avery has always come to my room. But after we heard the neighbors and she disappeared, I had to use the door."

Daniel shook his head, over and over. "Iris, you have to realize it now." He took a deep breath. "You've always had nightmares and they're just getting worse with the project. I mean, we *are* talking about graves, and looking up a lot of sad things. I think it's getting to you because you want the best project, or—maybe you're just ..."

Daniel looked so fearful, so serious, Iris was taken aback. She stared at him.

"Afraid."

The word hit Iris like a block of ice.

Iris pulled her jacket in closer. "I am *not* afraid," she muttered. She wasn't, was she? No. She went outside with Avery all by herself.

Iris squeezed her eyes shut. "That's not true. I'm not sleepwalking. Avery is coming to visit me because she understands that I don't want to be forgotten. She picked me to help her because I'm brave! She said there are few things she loves more than playing in the snow, just like me!"

Daniel stopped pacing and scoffed.

"You're finding yourself in the middle of the woods, making Vashti sad and lying to your mom."

"She needs my help, Daniel! She just—"

"Iris, we should've never gone to the clearing that night. That's when your dreams got worse! All of this is happening because you didn't want to follow the rules!"

Iris's eyes narrowed. She didn't know why she was feeling so angry toward Daniel. On the one hand, he was making a good point. But on the other . . .

"Is that what this is about? Me following the rules?" Iris asked him. "You're upset that I'm not being such a big rule follower like you?"

"Iris!" Daniel's eyes widened in shock. "How can you say that? It's not *just* about following the rules. It's about keeping you safe! I don't want to see you freeze to death! Plus, your parents specifically told you not to go to that clearing and you've been back already. Your dad had just told us the day before we both went the first time, remember? And our parents just told us again!"

Iris scoffed and rolled her eyes. "Gosh, Daniel! I'm not afraid, you are! You're afraid that I could actually be communicating with a ghost! When will you grow up and stop acting like such a baby?"

As soon as the words left Iris's lips, she tried to take them back.

"I—"

"Wow, I never thought *you*'d ask me that." Daniel looked down at his feet.

"Daniel, I'm sorry, I didn't mean to say that—"

Daniel backed up from Iris, his eyes glistening like ice in the sun. "I'll see you in class, Iris." He jogged a little ahead of her and walked the rest of the way to school.

"Daniel! Daniel!"

Iris watched as her very best friend walked away from her, leaving her feeling the coldest she'd ever felt.

CHAPTER 18

Daniel finally left the library, where he went after class to do some last-minute work on their project. His too-big book bag was weighing on his shoulders, on top of the fight he and Iris had.

Was he wrong? Was he wrong for being so cautious, for wanting Iris to be safe?

Daniel was only close to a few people, and had already lost one person. He almost lost another, his very best friend, last night, because she thought she was sneaking outside with a ghost.

He wasn't trying to tell her what to do—and deep down, he knew Iris knew that. But she called him a baby. Just like some of the guys at school did.

His eyes stung, which made him even more frustrated. The last thing he wanted to do was cry.

His house was only a few blocks away, then he could—

"Hey! Daniel!"

Oh no.

Daniel hastily pushed his glasses up to wipe the tear escaping his eye and walked a little faster to drown out the sound of his name.

"Daniel! I know you hear me, man!"

He heard a cluster of footsteps thump behind him before slowing down to a walk. On either side of him were two of his friends—if they could call each other that anymore—Jamal and Derek.

"'Sup, man?" Jamal said, holding out his hand for the usual handshake. Daniel dapped him up, firmly, just as his father always taught him, but didn't slow his pace. He was ready to go home.

"What's up," he murmured.

"We're about to go hoop down at the court. Want to come?" Daniel looked over to see Derek holding a basketball under his left arm.

"Not today, man. I—have to help my mom with something."

"You never hoop with us anymore!" Derek said, sucking his teeth. "What's going on—wait, are you crying?"

Daniel realized he was hunched over under the weight

of his book bag, and stood up straighter. Taller. "No, I'm not crying. It's cold. It gives me the sniffles."

"Oh. I was about to say. Because, if you were crying—"

"Look, I'll catch y'all later, okay?" Daniel said, his back aching under the pressure of his book bag. "My mom's waiting on me. I'll see y'all tomorrow."

"Dan, come on, man. When did you turn into such as mama's boy?" Jamal said, masking the disappointment, the sadness in his voice. "We miss you on the court!"

"Jamal, chill," Derek said, trying to catch Jamal's eye. And suddenly, Daniel knew what the unspoken words meant. *His dad died, so don't pick on him.*

"My mama needs some extra hands around the house now," Daniel said. Which wasn't entirely a lie. She would be happy for the help with dinner.

"Oh yeah, man, my bad." Jamal stumbled over his words. "I—uh—"

"I'll see y'all tomorrow," Daniel said again, not turning around when Derek chastised Jamal. He left a trail of two of his friends calling his name.

Derek, Jamal, and Daniel all hung out frequently, sometimes even calling on Iris when they needed to make the basketball teams even. But after Daniel's dad died, it was hard for them to really talk about it. They didn't know what to say to one another, didn't know how to talk about it. They were afraid of crying. Afraid of consoling. He knew it wasn't their fault. It seemed like they were all afraid of something.

They wanted him to come around more. Play basketball more like they used to. Hang out with Jamal's older brother, who Daniel didn't really like that much. He didn't like the stuff he did and he was pretty sure Jamal didn't either. But Jamal wanted to be like his older brother. Cool, mature, fearless.

Was Jamal doing to Daniel what Daniel was doing to Iris? Trying to change him?

But Daniel didn't want Iris changed. He just wanted her *safe*.

He walked home to find Suga intensely watching TV. His mom was still out; she'd told him this morning that she would be working late tonight to prepare for the big snowstorm coming in tomorrow.

"Hey, Suga," he said, taking off his coat and hanging it up.

"Oh, hey, baby!" she said, smiling widely at her grandson. Then she frowned. "What's the matter?"

He wondered if she could tell he'd been about to cry earlier.

"Nothing," he replied, trying to make his way to the kitchen to grab something hot to drink.

"Oh, don't give old Suga that. I know there's something wrong. Did something happen at school?"

Daniel sighed. He didn't want to get into his argument with Iris yet, but Iris tended to believe all of Suga's superstitions. Maybe if he could find a good one about leaving a ghost alone, he could tell Iris about it.

Whenever they talked again.

"Suga," Daniel asked, stopping in front of the kitchen, careful not to obstruct Suga's view of the TV. "Say—say someone was obsessed with a ghost. Or what they *thought* was a ghost. How would you get the person to . . . stop?"

Suga turned her head slowly to Daniel. He shifted on his feet.

"Maybe it's the other way around. Maybe the ghost is obsessed with the *person*," Suga said. "If that's the case, the ghost is attached to them."

"Well . . . okay. But how would you convince the ghost to leave them alone? To stop being . . . attached to that person?"

"Well, if a ghost is attached to a person, they've lost their way to where they were trying to go in the first place," Suga said. "You think a ghost would be happy, following a person around forever? No, they'd need to be led to where they need to go, so they can rest. A ghost obsessed with a person is a lost spirit."

Daniel thought of what Iris said Avery told her. *"I am lost and you found me."*

He shook the thought out of his head. This was not real. He was just looking for information to tell Iris.

"Well . . ." Daniel said slowly. "How long does it take a ghost to find where they need to go so they can leave that person alone?"

"Oh, Danny," Suga said. "The ghost has to be *led* away, some way or the other. That's why they've attached themselves to that person. They're hoping that person will guide them. In some rare cases, they can find what they're looking for and guide themselves."

Daniel's heart started beating faster. "You mean to—to their grave?"

Suga's stare pierced Daniel's. "Past their grave. *Beyond.* That's why I tell you kids not to play around outside at night. The spirits of the snow might latch on to ya!"

Daniel smiled shakily at Suga and wandered into the kitchen to make hot chocolate. So, he needed to convince Iris that Avery was a lost spirit trying to find her way "beyond," and if she needed to, she'd use Iris to guide her there. Which probably meant . . . killing her.

Daniel didn't believe any of this—it was just another one of Suga's superstitions—but he couldn't help but feel uneasy as he reached into the drawer and mistakenly grabbed a fork, instead of a spoon, to stir his hot chocolate.

He dropped it.

CHAPTER 19

Daniel sat down with his tablet and a notepad, trying to piece together everything Iris had told him about Avery. He'd relate it back to Suga's superstition, and that would for sure make Iris believe she should leave this idea of the ghost alone, and hopefully cure her nightmares and sleepwalking.

Iris's dreams and descriptions about Avery were pretty eerie: the eyes, her being lost, wanting a "forever" friend. But all of that fit into Suga's idea that Avery was attaching herself to Iris to kill her and lead both of them to rest.

Wait a minute.

Suga said Avery Moore was taken by the spirits of the snow. He didn't bother Suga again about it after seeing that she was so upset, but if she knew anything else, it could help their project and help Iris's dreams go away.

"My Lord!" A scream made Daniel jump so hard, he temporarily felt dizzy.

But it wasn't just any shriek.

It was Suga's.

"Suga! Are you okay?" Daniel asked.

"Danny!" she yelled as she looked out the window. "Do you see the way that snow's coming down?"

He looked out the window—the storm was coming in earlier than everyone predicted, a silent, violent force. He hadn't even realized it.

He walked toward her. "It's okay, Suga. Do you need anything?"

Suga said nothing, just looked out the window at the snow and ice, her face frozen in terror.

"Suga . . ." His heart was thumping.

"Yes, Danny?"

He sighed. He really didn't want to upset her.

"Suga . . . please don't get angry, but we need to know for our project . . . What happened to Avery Moore? Why did you say she was killed by the spirits of the snow?"

Suga looked at her grandson for a second, her lips trembling as she slowly got off the couch. She sighed, a heavy sigh that mimicked Daniel's. "I need to show you something. Come with me."

Daniel followed Suga upstairs to her room, which used to be the guest room and his father's old study. His desk was still there.

She opened the closet door and pulled out a thin book. The photo album they'd looked at together.

They sat on Suga's bed as she opened up the tattered, faded album to the first picture, of a young Suga—or Emma Mae back then—smiling and holding a melting ice cream cone in one hand, a basket in the other. She flipped past the other familiar pictures, of her getting her hair braided, pretending to sing . . .

They got farther in the photo album than they did before. In one picture, Suga was posing with a boy who looked like a taller version of Daniel . . .

"Lamar," she said, rubbing the picture. "Your grandfather."

Daniel could feel blood pumping in his ears. He looked like his Dad, too.

There was Suga laughing, a snowball in her hand, aiming at someone out of the picture. She was bundled up in a jacket, a hat, a scarf, and boots. There was so much snow on the ground. She looked so happy.

"Oh," Suga said, her voice and hand shaking. "I can't look at that." She hastily tried to shut the book again. Daniel stopped the book from closing with his hand and opened it back up.

There was another picture, of a younger Suga, standing with another snowball, with that same laughing face.

And beside Suga was another little girl, about Suga's height, laughing just as hard.

Daniel's stomach dropped as he stared at the girl's familiar face.

"Danny," Suga said, her voice cracking. "Avery was my best friend."

CHAPTER 20

Iris didn't have the energy to make it upstairs after step practice, which went by in a messy blur. She was consumed with her night with Avery, her fight with Daniel. They hadn't talked the rest of the day.

She knew she shouldn't have said what she said. She knew it was mean. But, as bizarre as the situation was, she was upset that her best friend didn't believe her. She knew she wasn't sleepwalking, or having nightmares about Avery. She was communicating with the girl's spirit. And last night, during their snowball fight, she'd actually had fun doing it. Avery did leave her out in the snow, by herself, but Iris got extra attention from her parents as a result.

"It's really coming down out there."

Her parents were bundled up, prepared to go outside in the slow but steady snowfall.

"Where are you going?" Iris sat up from where she was lying on the couch and looked anxiously to her mom and dad. She needed them here. She was too exhausted to deal with Avery coming again. "Y'all can't go anywhere in . . . the snow. It seems like the snowflakes are getting bigger by the second." She reminded herself of Suga.

"We'll be right back. We just need to run and get some things to prepare for the storm. It looks like it may be coming earlier that we thought," Mama said as they both kissed Iris and her sister. "We're going to divide and conquer so we can be back faster." If Iris weren't so afraid, she would've thought this was funny. It snowed in Easaw regularly enough for them to be used to it, but seldom enough that they felt the need to go out and buy milk and bread whenever there was a blizzard.

But instead of laughing, she lay back down on the couch and closed her eyes to catch up on some much-needed sleep.

"Y'all be good. And, Iris"—her mom knelt down beside her, lowering her voice to a whisper—"this would be a really good time to play with your sister."

Iris fought the urge to roll her eyes. How could she think about playing at a time like this? She was exhausted. Didn't her mom remember what happened last night?

Of course she didn't. She was probably too busy worrying about Vashti.

"See you in a bit, girls!" her dad yelled from the open door, letting the cold in. "Love you! Lock up!"

Iris ran to the door, locked it, and turned around to find Vashti standing right in front of her, grinning.

Iris jumped a little.

"Dolls?" Vashti said.

Iris sighed. She'd play for a little while and then be done with it. "Sure, 'Ti."

"Yay! I'll go upstairs and get them."

Vashti ran upstairs to get her dolls, already talking to them, using different voices. Her little sister had been upstairs for a long time now.

"Vashti, just come back down!" Iris yelled. She was getting impatient, plus Vashti talking to the dolls was giving her the creeps.

Her parents needed to hurry up. The wind was already whistling louder outside. The storm would be here soon.

The lights in the living room flickered.

Then went out.

With the curtains drawn and the storm picking up outside, Iris found herself in a pitch-black house. The dark, the thing she feared more than anything, was closing in on her.

"Vashti, hurry up!" Iris screamed, feeling around for the stairs.

She'd run to her room and get her flashlight.

She took the stairs two at a time, despite the dark. But when she reached the landing, she saw her:

Avery.

"Come, Iris Rose," Avery said. "Come with me, we will be remembered in a big way."

Iris was trying to fight it, but she could feel that force, pulling her somewhere.

"Vashti will be safe here. You did not want to play with dolls anyway. You wanted to rest. After my idea is done, you can rest. I promise."

Avery was right. Iris nodded, and let herself be taken away by Avery's cold wind.

She was lifted off her feet, then gone, the lights flickering back on moments later.

CHAPTER 21

Grief washed over Suga's face as she sat there, shaking her head.

"Suga." Daniel took his grandmother's hand. "Are you okay?"

She sighed and opened her eyes, smiling at the little sign of affection from Daniel. "I'm okay. I'm sorry . . . it's just your grandmother being weird again."

"I-I don't think you're weird," he said, his stomach churning with guilt. He didn't know she knew he thought that of her.

"Danny, I was born *at* night, not *last* night," she said with a dry chuckle. "Nothing gets past me. I see how you look at me when you think I'm saying something silly. Or when I don't know how to work your tablet or that big ol' TV remote downstairs. But it's okay. I thought my grandma was weird, too."

It didn't feel okay to Daniel anymore.

"Suga, I'm sorry."

"For what?"

"You're not weird. You're just—"

"Different? I'll take it." She smiled at Daniel, then frowned when she noticed the photo album was still in her hand. She sighed, a long sigh that carried so much weight.

"Suga?" He tried again. "What happened to Avery?" She looked at him.

"Our favorite thing to do was play in the snow. We stayed out all day, all night, until our fingers and toes were numb, just like you and Iris. She lived across the way."

Daniel knew that to mean she lived in an adjacent neighborhood from Suga.

"But my papa and mama had so much land in our old home, so we always played there. I lived right behind your school. For the majority of the time I lived there, Black kids weren't allowed to go there at all. Until Avery did. She was one of the first to desegregate the school. Some people in this here town loved that the school was finally open to Black children, and oh, Danny, a lot of people hated it. I should've told you about this, when you kids came over to talk to me ... but I didn't want to bring her up, Danny. I'm so sorry.

"The newspapers wouldn't even print those children's names at one time, did you know? They'd only say 'Nine Coloreds Desegregate Nelson's Pond Middle,' or something ridiculous. They deserved the same recognition Ruby Bridges got. They were so brave. I didn't want to join them. I was fine going to the school across the way, Dellerwood Middle. When I was younger, I'd walk by Nelson's Pond every day, knowing I wasn't allowed to learn there."

Suga sighed and closed her eyes. Then started again.

"One day, Avery and I got into a big fight—it's funny because I'll never forget it, but I *cannot* remember what we argued about. This was decades ago. Avery was so, so kind. Until you made her mad. We argued and she stormed away from my house—you know how dramatic you can become in a fight—and I sat there, stubborn in my feelings, and watched my best friend walk away for the last time."

Suga was crying now. Daniel thought of the argument he and Iris just had. How he had almost lost Iris to the snow last night. He had more in common with his grandmother than he thought.

"The snow started coming down, fast and heavy, and Papa made me come inside. If I had just stayed outside a little longer . . . maybe I could've saved her."

"What happened, Suga?" Daniel asked, still holding his grandmother's hand.

"Well, we didn't have cell phones or tablets or anything. That storm we had was one of the worst of the century—all of the papers were talking about it the next day—" She stopped herself.

"Suga?"

"Danny, Avery went missing! You'd think the officials would care, but I guess they felt they had more important things to do than worry about a little Black girl gone missing! Her parents came over and asked if we'd seen her and we said we hadn't. Papa told them she left to go home before the storm got too bad. Which was true. I remember that much. Well . . ."

Daniel gripped Suga's hand tighter.

"She died that day." Suga's lip was trembling more and more.

"My parents told me the story of the spirits of the snow. How they came and took Avery because she walked away, in the storm, by herself. My parents just told me that to keep me inside, to keep me from doing something foolish like Avery did. As I grew older, I knew the truth—Avery froze to death. They found her in the woods between my house and her house. It didn't make any sense because she left in enough time to get to her house before the storm really got bad. They think—they think she was on her way back to our house. To apologize."

Daniel's heart ached for Suga. There were no snow spirits after all.

Suga was sobbing quietly. "Danny, I never experienced loss like that before. And at such a young age! It makes me sad because . . . we never made up.

"The snow lost its appeal for me. I couldn't play in it without thinking about Avery. I was afraid that the spirits of the snow would get me, too. Her parents were mad at my parents because they thought we sent her home in the middle of the blizzard, instead of before it. I wasn't even allowed to go to her funeral. And do you know, Avery Moore, one of the first students to desegregate Nelson's Pond Middle, they buried her in a throwaway cemetery. I'd heard some whispers about it. Her family couldn't afford much else. She desegregated a school for crying out loud! And they . . . they wouldn't even tell me where she was buried!" she shrieked. "I lost my best friend to that stupid, stupid snow! I was never able to tell her I was sorry! I didn't want anything else to do with it. It took her from me!

"Danny, those years were a tough, tough time. I didn't go into it as I should've with you and Iris. It brings back a lot of bad memories. We were still able to have our joys, but boy, was there pain mixed in with it. After I met Lamar, we dated, got married, and moved to another house across town.

"Once I lost Lamar, and then your daddy . . . Well, I guess I let myself get swallowed up by the old superstition again. Everything felt so out of control. But I knew how to keep myself safe and that was by staying inside."

Daniel felt his eyes burn. He suddenly felt so, so sorry for Suga.

"But, Suga!" he said, sniffling. "You can't let fear control your life like that. Staying inside won't bring Avery, Grandpa, or Dad back. You're just taking away memories from your own life. You used to love snow. It's okay to be cautious, but you can't live your life in fear."

"It's the only way I could handle it, Daniel. She was my

best friend. There were few things she loved more than playing in the snow."

Daniel blanched; his bones chilled from the familiar words.

Iris had just told him that about Avery this morning.

Was it possible . . . ?

He shook his head. No, he was being silly. It was just a coincidence. He had to talk to Iris. He could let Suga talk to her about the superstitions, allow her to know the real girl who Avery was, not the ghost in her dreams. Suga could tell Iris herself that the spirits of the snow weren't real, and maybe that'd stop her nightmares once and for all.

And then . . . Suga losing her best friend to the snow without being able to apologize was too close of a situation for comfort. He and Iris needed to talk things out.

"Suga. Wait here. I'll be right back," he said.

"Where are you going?"

Daniel jumped, shocked at Suga raising her voice.

Her head snapped to the window, where the snow was coming down even steadier. "Do you see that weather? Do you see that snow, Daniel?"

"Just to Iris's, Suga," he said.

Suga's lip trembled. "Be careful," she said quietly. "Please."

"I will, Suga," he said.

She nodded, turning back to the window.

He walked downstairs, out of his house, to Iris's front door, then rang the doorbell. His heart was pounding in his ears. He couldn't help but feel that the information he just received was more urgent than even he knew.

He heard Vashti singing to herself before she came and opened the door. "Hi, Daniel!" She waved cheerfully, and walked back to playing with her dolls on the living room floor.

Alone.

"Hi, Vashti? Where's Iris?" he said, his heart thumping harder in his chest.

"Oh, she's not here," Vashti said casually, still playing with her dolls.

Daniel's heart dropped. "Is she with your parents?" he asked. He noticed their car wasn't outside.

"No. She left after them."

"Where did she go?" Daniel said, his voice shaking.

"She went somewhere with Avery."

Daniel couldn't have heard Vashti correctly.

"With . . . who?" he tried again.

"Avery. They left together earlier. I think Avery wanted to go swimming."

Daniel felt the room spinning like the snowflakes outside. He felt like he was in his own personal blizzard.

"Iris!" he yelled. He ran upstairs, throwing doors open, despite knowing he wasn't allowed up there. He opened her parents' room. Empty. Vashti's room. Empty, with the light on. Iris's room. Empty. Dark. The bed unmade. Her window open.

He ran back downstairs, looked around the kitchen, outside the window to the backyard.

Nothing.

He was about to run outside when he skidded to a stop in front of Vashti.

"Vashti," he said, breathing heavily. "How do you know Avery? Did Iris tell you that's where she was going?" Iris had convinced herself Avery was real, so she must've said it in her sleep, or before she sleepwalked outside, or—

Vashti put her dolls down and looked at Daniel, amused by his running around her house. "No! She told me herself. I like Avery. She wears a pink dress and has *biiig* black eyes," she said, stretching her arms wide. "She's like Sissy, but nicer. She played with my dolls with me when Sissy didn't want to anymore. She comes and has slumber parties with me at night. She looks really scary at first, but she's a great friend!"

Daniel's voice shook. "How did you meet her?"

"She comes to my room to play all of the time! Through the window!"

He felt sick. He thought of all the things Iris said to him about Avery. How she looked, how she was staring at her through her window . . . "When did they leave?"

"They didn't leave too long ago. Avery asked me if I minded if she went swimming with Iris."

"Swimming!" Daniel exclaimed, his voice shaking. "In this weather?"

"Avery *looooves* the snow." Vashti considered this and frowned. "But she'll keep Sissy warm, right?"

Daniel had to go after them. Now.

"Vashti!" he said, kneeling down and looking her straight in the eye. "Vashti, I'm about to leave. I'm locking the door behind me. Don't open the door for anyone besides me, Iris, or your parents, okay? If Avery comes back, tell her—to go away."

Vashti laughed. "Avery doesn't come through the front door, silly!"

Of course she doesn't.

"Just stay here."

Daniel couldn't take Vashti with him in this snow. He felt terrible about leaving her, but felt she was safer in here than where he was going.

Daniel knew what he had to do, but he was nervous.

It was getting darker.

Colder.

The snow was falling heavier.

He'd told Suga he was only going to Iris's. Now he was about to go somewhere he had no business being. He was about to do the very thing that got Avery killed in the first place. He knew that he should go inside and maybe call a grown-up. Do things the right way. But who would believe him? Besides Suga, and she would never agree to come out.

"Are you leaving now?" Vashti said.

"Yes, Vashti. I'm getting my best friend back."

CHAPTER
22

Every logical part of Daniel's body was telling him to run to his house and call his mother. He couldn't believe Avery was real. After all this time, she was truly haunting his friend.

He *hoped* they were still friends. Hoped this situation wouldn't become like Suga and Avery's. Where she'd never gotten to apologize.

Stop this, Daniel told himself. *You're not going to lose someone else you care about. Not like this.*

The storm seemed to be moving in faster than everyone predicted. It was dangerous for him to be out here by himself.

Which way should he choose? The careful way, or the brave one?

Why *did* he follow the rules so fiercely?

To stay safe.

Alive.

To respect the adults.

With every rule he broke, he saw the prospect of all three things leaving him. But Iris was not a rule follower, and she was out there somewhere. Maybe she was unconscious. Or cold. Or worse. By the time the adults got there and he told them where she was, it could be too late.

They were swimming, Vashti said. From what Suga told him, they had to be back at the pond.

He looked in the direction of his house, wondering if Suga was peeping out of the front door.

He needed to stay out of her line of sight. If he cut through the back of the house with all the Christmas lights, she wouldn't be able to see him leave. The only window facing this side of the street was the one in his bedroom. He could cut through the woods—the back way the other kids talked about that led to the school. And the pond.

He didn't let himself think the worst.

But he was worried.

His worry turned to anger as he thought of Avery, playing dolls with Vashti, leading Iris to danger, waiting for her parents to be gone to strike. She was evil, and he wouldn't be convinced otherwise.

Crunch.

Crunch.

Crunch.

Each step turned into a stomp. He was almost there, almost to the woods.

"Hey! Where do you think you're going?"

The voice yanked Daniel out of his thoughts, and he stopped in his tracks and looked around. A sheriff was leaning out of his car window as he drove slowly into the cul-de-sac, snowflakes sparkling in the beams of the headlights. He pulled the car to a stop just a few feet in front of Daniel.

Daniel sighed. This was just what he needed. He wanted to ignore him, to keep running toward Iris, but he knew that would only make things worse.

He stood still, saying nothing.

"Did you hear me? Where do you think you're going?" the sheriff repeated, his head sticking straight out of the window.

Act natural.

"I—" What should he say? He needed to hurry up. Every second counted for Iris.

"I'm going to my friend's house until my mom gets back from work."

It took everything in him not to grimace at his own lie. It wasn't a big lie, but he didn't like to lie and wasn't very good at it.

"In this weather?" the sheriff asked, raising his eyebrows. "This storm is picking up, you know."

Should he tell the officer the truth and have him look for Iris with him? Handcuffs and a gun were no match for a ghost, but maybe having an adult there would really make Avery leave Iris alone for good.

"Sir—actually, could you help me—"

"You wouldn't happen to know who's been messing around by that house, would you?" the sheriff asked Daniel.

Daniel blinked. "Excuse me? What house?"

"That one." The sheriff pulled his car even closer toward Daniel, pointing to the house with the lights. "We got a call that there were footprints back there. It could be an animal, but it could also be . . . a trespasser." He eyed

Daniel. "You wouldn't know anything about that, would you?"

Daniel's heart sank. It didn't seem like the sheriff would want to help Daniel. In fact, it almost seemed like he was *blaming* Daniel.

"No, sir," he said. "I don't know anything about it."

"Hmm," was all he said. "Well, the storm is picking up. You might want to go inside."

"Yes, sir."

And with that, the sheriff pulled off, leaving Daniel all by himself.

Daniel waited for the sheriff to finally turn around and drive off. Once the coast was clear, he carefully walked behind the neighbor's house with all the Christmas lights. He headed toward the clearing, just in case Iris and Avery were there, nervous about what he might find.

He arrived at the small clearing where Avery's grave and the others were buried under the snow.

This was the graveyard. Forgotten.

He looked around, anxious—half expecting to see a ghost pop out at him at any minute.

But there was no sign of Avery. Or Iris.

His heart sank. Then a flash of color caught his eye, and he spotted Iris's purple jacket, laid on top of Avery's grave.

He shivered and bent down to pick it up, to shake the falling snow from it.

"Iris?" he called out.

Nothing.

Why would her jacket be here if Vashti said she was going swimming? Shouldn't she be by the pond? Did they stop here first? Did Avery take her . . . beyond?

Daniel's fear turned into determination as he marched through the woods along the beaten path that some kids would take to school.

He was not about to lose his best friend to a ghost.

It was steadily getting darker, colder; the snow was falling so fast and hard into his glasses he debated just taking them off.

The wind whistled in his ears—it almost sounded like someone talking, yelling, screaming.

It was a short walk through the woods to the school, but the conditions made it impossible to see where he was going. He kept wiping his glasses with every step, his hood over his head. The leafless trees swayed, their gray branches looking like a million hands trying to grab him. His boots crunched on the snow, sticking to the ground, and he looked forward, behind him, up, and down as he walked. He shivered again as he tried his best to keep track of where he was, so he wouldn't get lost and meet the same fate as Avery.

Finally, he walked out of the woods, past Nelson's Pond Middle, straight to the pond itself.

Aside from the snow falling, there was no sign of life.

"Iris!" Daniel called out, wiping his glasses and squinting into the snow. He couldn't see a thing with or without them. "Iris!"

Where could she be if not here? "Iris!" he yelled again, running, stopping, looking. *Please let her be alive*, he prayed silently. He *couldn't* lose someone else. Not again.

"Iris," he said weakly.

He took a long, shuddering breath and ran toward the pond.

Then he saw it—saw her.

Iris's head broke the surface of the pond, her mouth open to take a loud gasp of breath, before she was pulled back underwater.

His eyes adjusted, letting him see the shimmering shadow of a girl forcing Iris's head back under, the face he'd only seen in pictures.

The face of Avery Moore.

He ran faster toward the pond, seeing Iris break the surface again, sputtering, coughing, trying to take another breath.

"Iris!" he exclaimed.

Iris and the ghost both turned to look at Daniel, Avery's black eyes causing him to yelp.

He made eye contact with Iris before Avery dunked her underwater again, longer.

This time, she didn't come back up.

CHAPTER 23

Avery wanted to kill Iris.

That was her big idea.

Because if Iris died, here, in this pond . . . when people would look for her, they'd first find the coat she left behind, leading them to Avery's grave.

Never mind that Iris had told Avery they were doing a big project on her, had planned to tell the school all the big things she did and restore the grave of Avery and the others.

Because this way, Avery told her, not only would she be remembered, but she really *would* have a forever friend. They could be ghosts together and do things together in a way that they couldn't with Iris still alive.

It wouldn't be so bad, Avery was trying to tell her as she fought against Iris, leading her to the pond. It would be fun.

But Iris knew better. Knew it was better to be alive, to present her project, no matter if she got the recognition she wanted or not. Because she would've done her part in getting history out there, the graveyard restored.

Knew it was better to argue with Vashti than have Vashti deal with losing her big sister. Knew it was better to play dolls with her. Knew the step team girls cared about her. Her parents, her friends, Daniel, even though they'd just argued.

But Avery wouldn't listen.

Instead, she'd pushed Iris into the pond and held her under. Iris tried to fight her, but couldn't, her arms going right through her instead. Avery used the same wind she'd used to make the snowballs to hold Iris down, the icy cold water shocking her body every single time she went under. She'd had to bite her tongue to hold in her scream. Get ready to breathe every time she was able to force her way out of Avery's grip.

She was getting tired, feeling numb.

But she'd heard her name.

"Iris!"

Someone was here.

She'd forced her way to the surface once more, barely making it this time, water getting into her mouth, making her cough.

It was Daniel!

She was plunged back down again.

Avery must've seen him, too, because she held Iris tighter . . . longer . . .

Until her vision went black.

CHAPTER 24

"Iris!"

Daniel slid on ice as he ran as fast as he could toward the ghost, to where his best friend was just dunked underwater.

Iris hadn't come back up yet.

Somewhere in the back of his mind, he was afraid. Afraid that he was going to be Avery's next victim. Afraid for Iris. Afraid to get caught.

He ran anyway.

Without a second thought, he threw off his jacket and his glasses and jumped into the pond.

The cold stung. Burned. Every part of him wanted to jump out and run back to the warmth and safety of his home.

But he couldn't do that without Iris.

He found her, swimming to the surface, fighting the invisible force that was holding her down, but he could tell she was getting weaker.

He swam toward her, his muscles tightening against his will. He grabbed her hand—yanked her from the force pulling her back, out of her trance—and they swam away, to another side of the pond.

Together, they broke free to the surface and tried frantically to swim to the edge of the pond, when Daniel felt a heavy push, and his head was shoved under the water. His lungs burned as he swallowed an icy mouthful. He flailed his arms and legs, not sure if he was bumping into Avery or Iris, but a moment later he was able to burst through the surface.

Only to hear Iris shriek as Avery pulled her back under.

Avery couldn't keep them both down at the same time, but she wasn't giving up.

So back and forth they went, Avery trying her hardest to hold down Iris, missing and holding down Daniel, giving Iris a chance to take another breath, until the two of them finally reached the edge of the pond, coughing, sputtering, heaving for air.

"Are you okay?" he asked his friend between coughs. It looked like her brown skin was tinted a shade of blue.

Iris just nodded. She was shivering uncontrollably.

He grabbed their coats, his glasses. "Iris, let's get out of here—"

"Who are you?" he heard a girl's voice behind him.

He was afraid to turn around, but willed himself to.

When he did, his eyes shook, his heart skipped a beat. A yell caught in his throat.

He was looking into eyes that were nothing. A transparent body that wasn't moving. Yet she spoke to him.

He was face to face with the ghost of Avery Moore.

He took in her shimmering figure, her stillness, the eyes Iris and Vashti described. He couldn't believe his *own* eyes.

But he needed to be brave.

"I'm Iris's best friend. Why are you t-trying to kill her?" he said loudly, his teeth chattered as he tried to gain the strength, the courage . . .

"She's *my* best friend now. Not yours."

"We got into an argument, but she's still *my* best friend!" Daniel yelled.

"*NO!*" Avery yelled back, her voice getting deeper. "She's *my forever friend*! No one will ever forget us again!"

Iris shook her head, still shaking, unable to speak from the near drowning she'd just endured for who knows how long.

Daniel narrowed his eyes. "Not if I can help it!"

Avery looked at him, her eye sockets growing bigger and bigger. He wanted to cover his eyes, but he didn't want her to know just how afraid he was.

She shrieked out of frustration. He flinched. She was just trying to scare him, trying to make him run away without Iris.

He wouldn't fall for it.

His heart was beating.

He quickly thought of what Suga told him earlier.

They're hoping that person will guide them. In some rare cases, they can find what they're looking for and guide themselves.

"Avery! I have what you want . . . what you really want! But you just have to leave Iris alone!" He didn't even know if that was true, but he was desperate. He walked closer to Avery, trying to lead her away from Iris.

"And what might that be?"

"You don't need Iris as a forever friend, when I know who your *true* best friend is! Her name is Emma Mae!"

Avery contorted her face in a snarl. She froze, still and cold as ice.

Iris looked at Daniel, her face covered in shock.

"Emma Mae, your best friend when you were alive!" Daniel yelled. "She's my grandmother and she thinks about you every single day!"

Had he said too much? What if Avery tried to drown Suga? Hopefully she'd guide herself beyond before that happened.

"Prove it!" Avery shrieked against the wind. "Prove it to me now!"

Iris was sputtering, coughing, crawling toward them. Avery whipped around, looking as if she was ready to drop her back in the pond.

"Not until you leave Iris alone!" Daniel glanced back and forth from the ghost to his friend, making sure that Iris was okay and that Avery wasn't trying anything new.

Iris rolled over on her back, her chest heaving.

She took a big breath and looked at Daniel, her teeth chattering so hard she could barely speak.

"L-l-light," Iris said. "She doesn't . . . l-like . . . l-light . . ."

Daniel quickly reached into the pocket of his jacket, pulled out the tiny flashlight on his keychain, and pointed it at Avery. She shrieked and floated backward.

"Bring me my friend, or else." Her voice was deeper than any he'd ever heard.

She was gone.

Just then, the wind increased, blowing so hard Daniel could barely stay on his feet. It whipped wildly around them, sending snow flurries into their faces and branches flying down from trees. Daniel had a feeling that it wasn't the storm picking up, but Avery conjuring up a wind to keep them from leaving.

"We have to get out of here," he said, helping his friend to her feet. She was still shaking.

He had no idea where Avery was, or if she was coming back, but he wanted to get Iris home before the storm got any worse. He had no intention of giving Suga to Avery. He had no idea what she'd try to do to her, where she'd try to take her, if she'd try to hurt her. If she tried to drown his grandmother and she survived, she would never leave her house again, snow or shine. And if she didn't . . .

He shook the thought out of his head. Avery wouldn't even get the chance. He wouldn't let her.

Together they pushed against the wind, walking slowly, silently, concentrating on each step. They bundled up as best as they could in their jackets, which were getting damp from the snow. The wind whistled louder and louder around them. "Argh!" Daniel screamed. He couldn't see a thing.

"Daniel!" Iris screamed, her voice faint and far away. They held each other tighter.

He felt like they were in a snow globe. He couldn't tell if he was walking toward or away from the pond. He could barely tell if they were right side up. "Keep holding my hand!" Daniel said. "We have to stay together!"

Daniel was shivering and so was Iris. He was so worried; she'd already been out here for a while, already been in the pond . . . it was too much cold for her. Avery was slowly trying to freeze her. They put their hands out, and soon they were touching trees. They were in the woods. He hoped they'd reach the clearing soon, but he wasn't even sure if they were going in the right direction. He wondered if this was where and how Avery died.

Daniel silently prayed, thought about his father. Thought about Suga. His mother.

Iris's hand was icy cold. He did his best to hold on, to not lose her in this snow.

"Please, please get us out of here," he whispered. He had no idea where they were.

Daniel saw a light. He let himself become relieved. He was starting to see houses!

But the light started blinking, a bouncing ball in front of them, illuminating their path.

"Come on!" Daniel said, walking toward it.

"No!" Iris screamed hoarsely. "What if it's a trap from Avery?"

Daniel couldn't explain it, but he didn't think so. He didn't feel afraid. This light felt like basketball and comic books and tying ties and haircuts. It felt like Sunday Night Football and weekend trips to the bookstore and sports documentaries.

"It's not," Daniel said confidently. "Let's go!"

They walked, following the bouncing ball. It led them through the intense windstorm around them. Daniel could see the woods, see the clearing, see the street they lived on.

"What *is* that?" Iris said as they approached the little ball. Iris stayed back, hesitant to touch it, but Daniel walked toward it, holding it in between his hands, giving it a bounce.

A familiar, warm comfort washed over him. He felt the excitement he used to feel from holding a basketball. He felt his dad telling him that it would be all right, that he was proud of him. That he was at peace.

"I miss you," Daniel whispered. "I love you."

The ball grew brighter, warmer, and Daniel knew the feeling was reciprocated. Then it dimmed, flowing slowly up to the sky until they could no longer see it.

Without the light, it was almost pitch-black. But they were in the clearing, facing their houses.

"Was that—" Iris gasped, her body shaking.

A tear fell from Daniel's cheek. "I think so."

Iris squeezed Daniel's hand. He squeezed it back, realizing again how cold she was.

"Iris?" Daniel asked softly. "Are you okay?" It was a silly question, he thought immediately afterward. Of course she wasn't okay. She was almost killed by an evil ghost.

"I'm . . ."

"What?" he asked, getting worried again. They were almost out of the clearing. The promise of a warm house and dry clothes led the way.

"I hate to admit it, but . . . I feel . . . afraid. What if you hadn't come in time?"

Daniel didn't want to think of that, of what could've happened.

Iris Rose, afraid. Daniel never thought he'd hear the words. As much as he wished he wasn't, he'd always been the afraid friend. Iris was the brave one.

"It's okay to be afraid sometimes," Daniel told Iris. "You're still a kid. It's okay." He paused. "I think you can be afraid of something and still be brave," Daniel said, thinking about his own experiences today. "I mean, I was afraid of looking for you today and breaking the rules, and—"

"And you still came looking for me. Even after our argument." Iris smiled a little, shivering less. "Thank you, Daniel, and I'm sorry. You aren't a scared baby."

"I think being afraid is okay as long as it doesn't stop you from saving your best friend from an angry ghost." He laughed, almost giddy with the thought that they were finally okay. "That's what best friends are for, right?

Finding each other when we get lost? You don't have to be brave by yourself *all* the time."

And with a start, he realized this was true. That they were really there for each other.

With that, Daniel's anger at Avery came back. His friend could've frozen to death in this snow, all because of Avery and her evil games.

They reached the end of the clearing and hurried through the neighbor's yard. Turned the knob to Iris's house.

It was pitch-black and silent.

"Vashti?" Iris whimpered.

She ran upstairs, calling her name. Daniel ran into the kitchen, back to the living room, looked in the foyer.

Vashti was gone.

CHAPTER
25

Iris ran from room to room upstairs while Daniel looked around downstairs, both of them screaming Vashti's name. Her heart dropped as she realized her sister wasn't there.

She wouldn't have left the house by herself, would she? Where would she go in this storm? There had to be some explanation—

"Sissy!" Iris heard Vashti's voice echoing through the house.

"Vashti?" Iris ran downstairs, but didn't see her. "'Ti? Where are you?"

She heard her little sister's voice amplified.

"Avery is taking me to her home to play in the snow! Just like she took you, Sissy!"

Iris's heart dropped. Avery?

"She just wants to be like her big sister," her mom was always telling her.

Iris wanted to pull her hair out.

Daniel ran from the foyer, back to the living room where Iris stood.

"She knows who Avery is, Iris," Daniel said quickly. "She—she's the one who told me you were with her."

"Where is she, 'Ti?" Iris cried. "Avery, show yourself and stop being a coward!"

"Oh, Iris Rose." She heard Avery's voice. "Vashti and I are working on *our* friendship. She wants to have fun, with someone who actually takes the time to play with her."

"Leave my sister alone," Iris growled. "Bring her back!" Iris felt dizzy, a snow globe shaken up too many times.

"Once I realized little Vashti Rose was here, waiting for the both of you to return, I suggested we play together. I do not like to be forgotten, Iris Rose."

Iris screamed in rage.

"Give me my real forever friend, and you can have Vashti back. Fail to do so, and I will have Vashti, forever."

"No, wait!" Iris screamed, running around the living room. "Wait!"

She heard nothing but her own ragged breathing. Avery was gone, and she'd taken her sister, the lights turning back on in their wake.

It all made sense now.

The shadows in Vashti's room, all the times that she heard Vashti talking and laughing with someone.

"Do you want to meet her?" Vashti had asked when Iris wanted to know about the "friend" her sister was laughing at.

"She's up there!" Vashti had cried when they were watching *Missy Mysteries*.

It was all Avery, all along.

The temper tantrum Vashti had after Iris was caught sleepwalking. She was so desperate to talk to Iris. She wanted to tell her something.

Avery had been pulling Vashti into this mess from the beginning. And Iris had been too busy to notice.

She was so upset about Daniel not believing her, but she had been doing the same thing to her little sister.

"My sister!" she wailed. "We have to get her back! How can we stop this?"

"Iris," Daniel said urgently. "I think there's a way to stop Avery, but . . ." He looked grim. "It's not going to be easy. I'll explain on the way."

She thought about what Daniel told Avery, about Suga. Remembered Avery's request to "bring me my friend, or else." She couldn't believe it. Would they have to choose between Vashti and Suga?

A violent chill rushed through Iris's body. They'd be no use to Vashti or Suga if they froze to death first.

Daniel studied her, shivering a little. "Are you okay? We need to ch-change out of these clothes."

Iris raced upstairs and grabbed both pairs of her Nelson's Pond sweat suits, one to give to Daniel.

Their parents. What if they couldn't find Vashti before their parents got back? How would they begin to explain this to them?

As she sprinted into the hallway, she felt a draft come from Vashti's room.

Her window was open.

Screaming in frustration, Iris ran into her sister's room and slammed the window shut.

"Iris?" Daniel called from downstairs. "Are you okay up there?"

Running downstairs, Iris nodded. She gave Daniel the sweat suit, then went into the bathroom to change before they bolted out of her front door.

"Iris," Daniel said as they hurried toward his house. "We have to convince Suga to come outside."

CHAPTER 26

"No."

"Please," Iris begged again, "we need you to come outside with us!"

"Suga! We have to! I know it's scary, but you have to listen! Vashti—" Daniel tried.

"Daniel, I told you! I don't go out in the snow!" She only called him Daniel when something was final.

"Suga, I need you to listen to me, and don't panic, okay? Avery Moore has Vashti!"

She looked at the two of them.

"What did you just say?"

He grabbed Suga's hand and they told her together how they started communicating with Avery, what happened with Iris in the clearing, in the pond, in the blizzard, and now with Vashti. How she needed to be remembered.

They were talking fast, words spilling over each other, but they didn't have any time to waste.

"We know this sounds impossible, Suga, but please believe us! It could be too late, and Avery only agreed to leave Iris and Vashti alone if we showed Avery her real friend. Remember what you told me earlier? *You're* the thing that she's searching for. This could be the only thing to save Vashti and make her leave us alone for good!" he concluded.

Suga sat, her eyes wide, her mouth open, looking back and forth at the two of them, probably trying to decide if it was a joke, or just a dream, or just their imaginations getting the best of them. Daniel knew it was a lot for her to take in at once, a lot to believe—he didn't even believe it until he saw Avery with his own two eyes—but with every moment they waited, Vashti could be in more danger.

But if anyone would believe them in a hurry about the supernatural, it was Suga.

"Oh my goodness," Suga said. Her face looked pale. "My goodness, my goodness . . ."

"Suga," Daniel said, squeezing his grandmother's hand.

"Suga ... This is your chance to finally make peace with Avery! To tell her your side of the story and let her know that you're here!" Iris pleaded.

"Daniel ... are you sure this is really her and not some other ... spirit?" Suga asked slowly. "The Avery I knew was kind and wouldn't hurt anyone."

"I think she grew cold with years and years of feeling like she'd been forgotten," Iris said quickly. "She doesn't remember who she used to be. Now she's trying anything she can to be heard."

Suga closed her eyes tightly, like she was having an internal battle. She sighed.

"Okay."

Daniel and Iris helped bundle Suga in sweaters, a jacket, and scarves. There was no time to lose.

"Don't worry, Suga! We will *not* let her take you," Daniel said forcefully.

"I'm not worried about that," Suga said. "If this is really Avery, she'd never hurt me."

Daniel wasn't too sure.

"Vashti said Avery was taking her home, I assume to her grave," Iris said, her voice cracking.

At least, she hoped so.

The three of them ran as fast as they could, trying not to slip, leading Suga, who was transfixed by the snow around her. She looked at everything like it was new: the snow on the ground, the ice in the trees. Every time one of their boots crunched a little too loudly on the snow, her head would jerk in that direction.

They approached the clearing and saw no one.

"She's not here!" Iris wailed. Avery must've suspected they'd come here first. If something happened to Vashti because of her, she'd never forgive herself. She pictured herself becoming like Suga, cursing the snow at every chance she got. She was scared and wanted her sister back more than anything.

She thought back to the night that started everything. The night when they first came to the clearing and made the snow angels.

That was it.

"Suga," she said. "Suga. I think you need to make a snow angel right there. That's how I summoned her."

Suga stared at Iris like she was the ghost.

"Right there? Why?"

"Suga," Daniel said, taking a deep breath. "Suga . . . this is where Avery's body is buried."

Suga looked at Daniel and Iris. Her chin trembled.

"It is?"

Iris and Daniel nodded, then took each one of Suga's arms, helping her kneel down to look at Avery's grave.

She wiped the snow from the grave marker and stared at it.

"My goodness," she said. "After all these years."

Suga closed her eyes, tears falling from her cheek.

"It was right under my nose the entire time."

It seemed like there was so much that they missed that was right under their noses.

After a moment, Daniel knelt down beside his grandmother and hugged her. "It's okay, Suga."

Suga closed her eyes and started to lie on the snow. Daniel and Iris helped her.

"Think, Suga," Iris said. "Think of those moments that you have tried to forget. With Avery."

Suga's chin trembled, but she closed her eyes again, and thought.

Meanwhile, Iris closed her eyes and thought of Vashti.

'Ti, if you come back, I'll play dolls with you every day during winter break. We can wear our matching nightgowns and have step shows and—

"Keep thinking, Suga," Daniel said.

There was silence, for a second. Then, with a strong gust of wind, blowing snow everywhere, there were Avery and Vashti.

Suga gasped loudly, crawling away. "Avery?" she asked. She looked at her, fear covering her face. Iris realized how strange it must be for Suga to see Avery as a ghost. Daniel helped her to her feet.

Avery whipped around. "Who are you?"

"Avery, it's me," Suga said, walking toward her slowly, still staring at her. "It's Emma Mae. We were best friends. I remember you."

There was silence as Avery regarded Suga.

Vashti ran to Iris and hugged her close. Iris hugged her back tightly, wrapping her inside her puffer coat. They shivered together, trying to warm each other up.

Suga muttered something that looked like a prayer, then took a step toward Avery.

"The Avery Moore I knew was kind and strong. She wouldn't let anyone change that, no matter what she went through. She did great things. But what you're doing, hurting children to be remembered ... you've been so upset that you don't even remember who you are anymore."

She took another step.

"The last day you were alive, we argued at my house by the pond. You left, and our families were upset with each other because of it. Because of how you died. But, Avery, you've always been my best friend."

She took another step, until she was right in front of Avery.

"Do you remember me?"

Avery looked at Suga, unmoving. Iris was nervous. She hoped this worked. She hoped Avery wouldn't try to hurt Suga.

"I remember light ..." Avery whispered. "And snow-ball fights ... ice cream shops ... Popsicles on the front porch ..."

"Yes," Suga said. "What else?"

"Parents who loved me ... swimming in the pond ... nice boys who bagged our groceries ..."

"One turned out to be my husband and Daniel's grand-father," Suga said, a smile on her lips. "Go on."

"Learning in school despite the odds . . . my best friend . . . Oh, Emma!" Avery's voice trembled. "Is it really you?"

"Yes. It's me!" A tiny laugh escaped Suga's mouth. "It's me. Daniel is my grandson, and Iris is his best friend."

She turned back to Suga, suddenly taking in the age difference between them.

"Who did you marry?"

"I married Lamar Stone. Fifty of the best years of my life."

"*Lamar Stone?* No wonder he always stuck something sweet in your grocery bag!" Daniel's granddad was the same age as Suga but used to help out in the grocery store with his father on weekends.

The two of them chuckled. Iris just stared at them. Vashti clung to Iris, squeezing her legs tighter.

Daniel was frowning.

The laughter hung in the air, Suga's smile fading.

"She almost drowned Iris." Daniel spoke up, and every-one looked at him.

"Yeah," Iris added, anger welling up inside her. "And left me in the clearing, trying to make me die in a snowstorm like she did, and *kidnapped Vashti*."

"Avery?" Suga asked, looking uncomfortable again, shaking her head.

"I wanted to get justice. Vashti was more than willing to play and be my friend . . . and I knew that if Iris or Vashti was missing . . . it would lead people back to me and my grave."

Suga shook her head. "That's not you."

"Avery didn't care if anyone died so she could be recognized!" Daniel said. "She tried to kill them herself! That's a terrible thing to do!"

"Danny's right, Avery," Suga said solemnly. "The children are already working hard to make your grave known."

Daniel just crossed his arms.

Avery looked at Suga.

"Emma?" Avery said quietly. "I am sorry for our argument. I don't even remember what we were arguing about. But I died trying to tell you, and I wanted to finally tell you that I truly apologize."

"*You're* sorry? *I'm* sorry! I blamed myself!" Suga said, tears falling down her cheeks. "It was all my fault that you died. We should've never argued. Your parents hated me after that!" She wiped her eyes. "I forgive you, Avery, but it's not only me you have to apologize to. You've had these children worried sick about each other and Vashti. What you're doing is disgraceful."

Avery turned and glided toward Iris. Iris backed away, still not entirely convinced.

"Iris Rose, I'm sorry for everything. I understand that I shouldn't have played with Vashti . . . although we did have fun playing with dolls, did we not?" she added, and Vashti giggled. "Emma Mae is right, I have grown cold."

Iris sighed a long heavy sigh, releasing the anger she felt toward Avery. Trying to understand that though her tactics were reckless, and she was lost in her anger, guilt, and bitterness for being forgotten, she was trying to find her way out. "I forgive you, too, Avery."

Avery turned to Daniel. "Daniel, I—"

"*NO!*"

Everyone jumped as Daniel's voice rang through the clearing.

"You almost killed my best friend! And her little sister! Do you understand?" Daniel exclaimed. "I lost my dad. I didn't want to lose anybody else. I understand you wanting to be remembered. But you put us all in danger. If we weren't quick enough, we could've lost them both tonight."

"Daniel, you have a right to be angry," Avery said.

Daniel closed his eyes and breathed in and out.

"I do apologize, Daniel," Avery said. "You don't have to forgive me."

The clearing was silent for a while as they looked at one another, at Daniel.

Iris had never known Daniel to hold a grudge for too long, but . . .

"I'm *not* over it." He looked at Avery. "I was also a little . . . jealous."

"Jealous?" Avery, Iris, and Suga asked in unison.

"Of what?" asked Iris.

"I dunno. I guess . . . well, Avery came back to talk to Iris, but why can't my dad come back to talk to me? Except for—" He stopped, probably thinking about the bouncing ball of light that led them back to safety. Or his dreams.

"Danny, you know we don't call on the dead." Suga looked at Daniel pointedly, then at Avery. "Well, after this we won't. Cecil is at peace. Avery is *a spirit not at rest*."

"At peace," Daniel said thoughtfully.

"I want that for you, Avery," Suga said as she looked at the ghost. "It's been too long! We've apologized to each other. Go. Please. Rest. We'll have your love. And you'll have ours."

"And . . . you have my forgiveness," Daniel said.

Everyone looked at him.

Daniel peered at all of them and adjusted his glasses. "There's no point of being mad anymore if Avery's leaving us alone. Suga seems to trust her . . . and everyone's safe."

Avery beamed. It seemed as if light was coming out of her, instead of darkness.

Avery turned to Suga again. "So . . . they call you Suga? That's lovely."

"Everybody does," said Suga. "When my son was a baby, I would always call him Sugar and he'd always say it back to me. It just stuck."

Avery looked back and forth between Daniel and Suga. "I know you miss him."

They both nodded.

"I think about him every day," Suga said.

"So do I," said Daniel.

"Think about him being at peace," Avery said.

Everyone nodded and stood in silence again. Vashti was getting fidgety.

"Emma Mae, you'll always be my best friend," said Avery. "I can feel your love." She gave Suga a slow smile. "I have what I need."

If Iris wasn't mistaken, she could see the gray tint leaving Avery's skin, the dark cast leaving her eyes.

"Goodbye," Suga said, smiling through her tears.

"So long," Avery said, and with a gust of wind and a twinkle of light, she vanished.

For a long moment, the four of them stood there, looking down, up, around, saying nothing. The heavy snow let up, and the wind had stopped blowing. The clouds opened up, and Iris could see the stars twinkling high above in the cold night sky. The little clearing was lit with the light of a glowing moon.

"This is my first time feeling snow on my skin in years," Suga said, holding her hand out and touching the snow.

"Well, we might as well go all out, right?" Iris said. She scooped up a big handful of snow and started making a snowball.

"Yeah!" Vashti said, following suit.

"Suga?" Daniel held out snow in his hand to give to Suga. She took it.

"Oh, why not?" she said, shaping the snowball . . .

And throwing it at Daniel.

As the four of them ran into the street, throwing snowballs at one another, Avery's grave twinkled, ever so slightly.

CHAPTER 27

"Are you nervous?" Daniel asked.

Today was the day they presented their project. The project they'd worked so hard for, literally risked their lives for, was finally about to *come* to life.

It was the last full day before winter break, and since the project was kind of a big deal, Mr. Hammond said they could invite their family members. So, sitting in class, along with everyone else's parents, were Mama, Daddy, and Vashti, Mrs. Stone and Suga.

Last week, when Suga came into Iris's house after they talked to Avery, covered in snow... the Roses and the Stones didn't know what to think. But they were happy. And Suga vowed to come watch Iris and Daniel present their project.

"Not really," Iris answered Daniel. "I'm more ready to get this story out... and get this over with."

"Same here," Daniel said, nodding. "Let's do it."

Iris sniffled, glad that she was getting over the lingering cold she'd gotten from way too much cold water and air. She plugged in her flash drive and pulled up the file, showing the title slide of the project:

FORGOTTEN: THE HISTORY OF
SEGREGATED GRAVEYARDS IN EASAW

The class murmured, oohed, and aahed when they read it. Heather had just presented her project on the Confederate soldiers of Easaw and passed the sword, her family's heirloom, around the class.

They each took out the index cards they were reading off of, to prevent them from having to look back at the slides so much.

"Today, we are talking about the segregated graveyards in Easaw," Iris started. "Although segregated cemeteries were already around before this, the *Plessy v. Ferguson* decision of 1896 made it legal to bury people separately according to race. This became North Carolina law in 1947, as legislation enacted 'Use of cemeteries for burial of dead, according to race.' This happened, particularly in the South, until the Civil Rights Act of 1964 took effect. Even in Easaw."

"Because of this," Daniel continued, "when the original caretakers of these cemeteries fled North, a lot of these cemeteries were forgotten about and disturbed as people built buildings and highways on top of them. Here in Easaw, there is one in particular that Iris and I found while doing our research. And it was very literally right in our backyard."

Iris picked up. "Right down the street, there was an abandoned cemetery, blocks away from Sampson's Perpetual Care, which was originally for Whites only. Although Sampson's Perpetual Care has been desegregated for decades, the unnamed Black cemetery down the street was left to be forgotten about."

"My father is buried in Sampson's Perpetual Care," said Daniel, a little quietly. Then, clearing his throat, speaking louder, "Had he been born and died a few decades earlier, he wouldn't have been allowed to."

Iris clicked to the next slide, showing a black-and-white picture of nine students.

"These children are the Nelson Nine, or the first Black students to attend Nelson's Pond Middle in 1955," said

Daniel. He slowly named them, one by one. "Before them, this school that all of us attend right now was for White students only. The desegregation of this school was not well received by many, and because of this, there isn't much mention of the Nelson Nine anywhere. If you noticed, they aren't even on the Hall of Fame wall. On the internet, there is nothing that Iris and I found. This picture is from a book in our library."

"Avery Moore is the fourth girl in the first row," Iris said, the name bringing back so many memories. "Although she made history by desegregating this school, she died tragically in a snowstorm when she was eleven years old. Almost our age! She was buried in the unnamed cemetery down the street. Her grave was eventually lost to the woods."

Some of the classmates gasped.

"We have talked to someone who was very close to Avery, and we learned that she was not the type of girl who'd want to be forgotten, especially after what she'd accomplished," Daniel said. "Namely, that person is my grandmother Emma Mae Stone, who's here today."

The class turned around in their seats to look at Suga, who merely smiled and nodded her head.

"Daniel and I are very passionate about cleaning up this cemetery and honoring those who were laid to rest there. And because of this, we have submitted the idea of a cemetery cleanup to the Cleanup Club to start an ongoing project of restoring the cemetery," Iris said, grinning. "The information meeting will be today, after school is out. We have flyers about the club and what we want to accomplish, so pass it along to your friends."

Iris and Daniel walked around the class, passing out the flyers to students and parents.

"We know that this isn't the only abandoned and segregated cemetery in Easaw," Daniel said, "but we hope that it starts a change—restoring these cemeteries and bringing them to your knowledge. We hope that our project serves as a way to never forget those who have paved the way before us, and encourages everyone to always strive to make a difference."

The class applauded, as did Mr. Hammond. Iris and Daniel walked to where their families were sitting and sat down.

"How did we do?" Iris asked her parents as Vashti jumped in her lap to give her a hug and kiss.

"Amazing," Mrs. Rose said. "Iris, I am so proud of you."

"My girl," Mr. Rose said, kissing her on the cheek. "You did so well. Y'all were the best," he added in a whisper, and Iris giggled.

"Daniel, your father would've been so proud," Mrs. Stone said. Daniel blushed, fidgeting with his glasses.

"I just want to say thank you both. For *everything*," Suga said. She winked. Only the kids really knew what she meant.

"All in favor?"

Everyone raised their hands, except Heather.

"It's settled. Our first cleanup at the cemetery will be this Saturday for the kids who are still in town during winter break. Then we'll go every Saturday afternoon at four p.m. until it's completed. The information and update meetings will start on a new day and time next semester, ensuring that it doesn't conflict with any other after-school activities. There will be more to come during the morning announcements."

Iris and Daniel looked at each other and beamed. Not only did their project get picked up, the meetings were no longer happening during step practice.

It was after school, and the Cleanup Club meeting had just wrapped up. A few kids showed up to join the club, including the entire step team. Even Daniel's friends Jamal and Derek came, and Daniel was in the corner of the classroom with them, talking and catching up.

"I hope you're pleased with yourself," Iris heard someone grumbling in her ear. She turned around to find Heather, sneering at her.

"As a matter of fact, I am," Iris said, raising her eyebrows. "How could you possibly be unhappy about this? A grave getting restored? Someone who did something amazing for the school getting recognized?"

"My father says this must be political. Is your father running for mayor or something?"

"Huh? I—no?"

"Chelsea probably felt pressured to vote for your project because everyone else did. Y'all just come bombard your way into this club—"

"Isn't the club for anyone who wants to join, at any time?" Iris said, not feeling as riled up as she normally would've. Her mom was right—you just couldn't please everyone.

Speaking of, Iris saw her parents walk into the classroom with a woman holding a microphone and a man holding a camera. When they saw her, they waved her over.

"Hold that thought," Iris said, leaving Heather and walking to her parents. What were they doing here? Iris and Daniel usually walked home after school.

"What's going on?" Iris said, walking toward them.

"I'll grab Daniel," Daddy said to Mama, and came back in a few seconds with him.

"I'm Samantha Evans," the woman with the microphone said. "We're with WEAS Nightly News, and we wanted to talk to you kids about the cleanup you two organized."

Iris's eyes opened so wide, they almost popped out of her head. "*Us?* Really?"

"Yes," the woman said, her smile warm and friendly. "It's so nice what you're doing for the community. We want to spotlight that, and document the progress of the cleanup. Is that something you'd be interested in? We just want to talk with you on where you got the idea and what you see for the future of the cleanup."

Iris didn't know what to say. It was happening! It was really happening! She was actually getting recognition for something she did.

"We'd love to!" Iris said, and Daniel nodded, fixing his glasses.

The reporter smiled again. "Awesome. Let me just grab the mics for you." She walked off.

Mrs. Rose looked at Iris. "I told you, in due time, sweetie," she said. "For you and Avery."

Iris smiled.

Mrs. Rose furrowed her brow. "I meant to ask the two of you, but . . . what made you so invested in this project in the first place?"

Iris opened her mouth, closed it, and opened it again.

The truth.

"Mama, would you believe me if I told you Avery visited me herself and told me? But now she's happy and at peace?"

Mrs. Rose looked at her daughter and smiled. "I wouldn't doubt you. I've had a ghostly encounter before when I was younger."

Iris's eyes spread wide. "Really?"

Mrs. Rose winked. "Iris Michelle Rose, that's a story for another day."

CHAPTER 28

CHRISTMAS DAY

Iris loved Christmas dinner—after waking up that morning to presents in matching plaid Christmas pajamas with her family, it was time for Daniel and his family to come over for one of her favorite meals of the year. Her parents did this together: fried turkey, macaroni and cheese, cornbread, mashed potatoes, green beans, and that wasn't even including the Christmas desserts, and a fresh batch of chocolate chip cookies (if her dad didn't eat them all).

It was snowing very lightly, not the kind that would stick, but the perfect backdrop for a Christmas evening.

The doorbell rang. "That's probably Mrs. Stone and Daniel," Mrs. Rose said, walking to the front door.

"Oh my—what a lovely surprise!"

Iris didn't want to get her hopes up, but she did anyway, and grinned. She knew Suga would come. Sure enough, she walked in behind Daniel and Mrs. Stone.

"Suga!" Mr. Rose said. "We're so glad you could join us!"

"Of course I'd come! Why waste any more time being afraid? There's a whole world out there." Suga winked at Iris, Daniel, and Vashti. They giggled.

"And I couldn't pass up Christmas dinner!" she added. "I hope y'all have enough food for me."

"Plenty," said Mrs. Rose. "Have a seat! It's almost ready."

"I got some hot cocoa for you two," Mr. Rose said, handing two marshmallow-topped mugs to Daniel and Iris. "And chocolate milk for Vashti. Would y'all like anything?"

"I think we'd like some tea, thank you!" Mrs. Stone said, Suga nodding in agreement.

Daniel and Iris sat together, sipping their cocoa. The hot drink made Iris feel warmer inside than she already did.

"Tomorrow," said the newscaster on the TV as the Christmas movie they were watching went to commercial, "the Nelson's Pond Middle school Cleanup Club's process on the abandoned, segregated cemetery is continuing, with a ceremony next week, dedicating the cemetery as Avery Moore Perpetual Care."

"Oh, look!" Mrs. Stone said. "And there's you, Daniel . . . and Iris! Look, that's all of us! On TV again!"

Sure enough, the camera cut to different pieces of footage, including shots of the seven of them helping to restore the graveyard.

"Although it has been difficult to locate the names of all those who are buried here"—Iris saw herself on TV—"we now have the help of Easaw's Department of Archives and History to match up the more difficult ones. This process will be long, but we are at least excited to dedicate the cemetery with the new headstones donated by Sampson's Perpetual Care."

"Some families have even been reunited with loved ones that they assumed were lost forever," the newscaster continued.

"My grandmother always told me the stories of my great-uncle Henry. When I found out about this cleanup, I knew there was a strong possibility he was buried there," a woman holding a newborn baby said. "This has been monumental for our family."

Iris thought about a grave marker she saw—Henry. She smiled.

The newscaster appeared back on TV.

"The Nelson's Pond step team will be hosting a fundraising step show to continue to raise funds for the cemetery. There will be more information on this on our website, and tonight at eleven."

Suga sighed contently.

"Oh, I am so thankful," Suga said, and Mrs. Stone nodded. "So, so thankful."

"That I am, too, Suga," said Mr. Rose, setting down two mugs of tea in front of Suga and Mrs. Stone. "That graveyard is *historical*. I'm glad those buried and their loved ones are getting what they deserve."

"Me, too, Daddy," Vashti said. Mr. Rose raised an eyebrow at her.

"What? I care about the neighborhood!"

"And I don't doubt that for a second, sweetie," he said, hugging her. She laughed, a chocolate milk mustache shining on her face.

"Dinner is served!" Mrs. Rose yelled from the kitchen.

"Great. I'm starving!" Iris said, getting up from the couch, hot cocoa in hand.

"That's great about the graveyard," Daniel whispered as they walked to the dining room. "You know, I hope Avery is at rest."

"I think she is. I just have a good feeling about it," said Suga.

Iris stood around the table, holding hands with Daniel and Suga, preparing to bless the food. She was sleeping a lot more soundly at night. She knew the twinkle she felt in the clearing was the last one. It didn't feel urgent or scary, but calm, warm, and happy.

When she'd visited Avery's newly restored grave and saw the cool winter sun peeking through the trees, the light dancing on the snow, she'd known. And whenever she'd see it again, as long as she lived, she'd always remember.

AUTHOR'S NOTE

Dear Reader,

I have two family members, Uncle Sammy and Great-Aunt Beatrice, buried in Randolph Cemetery in Columbia, South Carolina. This cemetery was for African Americans only. After the Great Migration, when African Americans in the early 1900s moved to the North, Midwest, and West to escape the intense segregation in the South, the cemetery became overgrown and abandoned—the same way Avery's grave did. In 1959, the city arranged for the cemetery to be cleared out in an urban-renewal program. A bulldozer was allowed to clear out the cemetery, and it destroyed some of the graves in the process! Luckily, a woman by the name of Minnie Simons Williams drew attention to the historical significance of the cemetery and brought a stop to the clearing of it. From there, she and descendants of the founders of this cemetery established the Randolph Cemetery Association to restore and maintain it.

I heard bits and pieces about this cemetery from my grandmother growing up and was shocked that segregated cemeteries existed. I learned that there were many of these cemeteries around the country and wondered how many were still abandoned.

I was also shocked by the story my grandmother told me about the grave markers of my late uncle and great-aunt: That, over time, the grave markers slowly began to rotate, until they faced each other. I've seen them myself! These pieces of information had my mind buzzing and made me want to write a ghost story.

Like Iris, when I was younger, I was in a situation where I won an award (ironically, it was a school-wide award for writing!) but didn't get to attend the ceremony because I was never told about it. I was disappointed, of course. I felt forgotten. But writing was more important to me than being recognized by people who may or may not have wanted to see me win. So I kept writing. And now look— I've published my first book! Missing that ceremony doesn't even bother me anymore. Recognition can be great, but as Iris's mom says, it isn't everything. And you don't have to go looking for it. By working super hard at what you love, it'll eventually find you.

I hope you enjoyed *The Forgotten Girl* and found it to be spooky, inspiring, and informative. I worked hard on this book, and I'm so thankful that you took the time to read it.

India

ACKNOWLEDGMENTS

First off, I'd like to thank God and Jesus, for putting this dream in my heart to be an author for as long as I can remember, for making the path to my first novel better than I ever could've imagined, and for connecting me with Holly the day I prayed and needed a sign to keep writing. I'm forever grateful.

To Holly Root, my literary agent: THANK YOU for taking the chance on me as an author, understanding exactly the type of author I'd like to be, and always having my best interest at heart. You are amazing. and I'm so thankful for you.

To Emily Seife: I could not have asked for a better editor. Thank you for being patient with my many questions, and helping to make this story the best version that it could be. I'm so grateful to be working with you.

The Scholastic team: I remember poring over the Scholastic Book Club catalog, circling the books I wanted.

Sometimes it still feels surreal to be publishing with you. Thank you for the opportunity, and for that special "Book Fair" feeling that I will never forget. To Maeve Norton: Thank you for designing the cover that I love, that feels so perfect for this story. Josh Berlowitz, Kerianne Steinberg, Elisabeth Ferrari, Rachel Feld, Lizette Serrano, and Emily Heddleson: Thank you for all your help in bringing this story to life.

To my husband, Rob: Thank you for replying "Why not?" when I asked you if you thought I could write a ghost story. You support me through all my ideas, stories, and endeavors, remind me to write when I'm procrastinating, and always provide a listening ear to my many, many rambles.

To Mommy: Thank you for always making me feel like I could pursue the career that makes me happy, and never judging me when I quit perfectly good jobs to do just that. Thank you for always pushing me and Eli to follow our dreams.

Ma, thank you for being my own personal Suga, a feisty grandma with all kinds of superstitions. You bring everyone so much joy.

Aunt Annette and Uncle Lamont: You have supported me in so many ways throughout the process of me writing this book! I'm so thankful. And before you say anything silly . . . "Shut up, Lamont!"

Olivia and Antonio: Make sure you tell everyone at school that your name is in this book. Always follow your dreams, even if they seem hard at first.

To my little brother, Eli: Thank you for being you.

Uncle Tony: I know you are smiling down on us, and I hope I'm making you proud. Thank you for the Harry Potter series you bought me, which ignited my love for them.

Devon, Uncle Greg, Uncle Shawnelle, Deshawn, Alex, Rochele, Ced, Tristyn, Marcel, the entire Hill family: I love y'all. I don't know of any family closer than us! This book is largely about family, and that's thanks to you.

To my mother-in-law, Kelley, and Aunt Tracey: Thank you for your continuous support and welcoming me into your family during the time this book was being written!

To the Hollidays and the Schofields: Thank you for the countless trips to the bookstore growing up, and supporting my love for reading.

KaShawn, thank you for always supporting me as a writer! I feel like you were there every step of the way through this process, from beta reading to bouncing ideas off of. You're the greatest best friend, and I cannot thank you enough!

To my Besties: Tee, Ciera, and Nia. For all the laughs and support for the past eleven (!!!) years and counting! I'm so thankful for your friendship.

To Delta Sigma Theta Sorority, Inc: I'm so happy to be a part of such an incredible sisterhood.

To Claflin University: Thank you for focusing me and helping me to love writing again.

To the Fellows: Jeremy, Marissa, Charlie, and Rachel. Rachel, thank you for printing my manuscript whenever I asked.

To my mentor, Alexa Donne, for always being there for advice during some really pivotal moments in my career. I'm so grateful to have you as a mentor!

Nic Stone, for always being supportive and reaching out to me as a new author. Dhonielle Clayton and Renée Watson, for writing amazing books and being role models. Karen, Lisa, Mariama, and Alicia, for navigating the debut world with me! Shannon Dittemore and Kayla Olson, for sharing in our love for Jesus and writing.

For Robin Lowry, who I knew as Ms. Drucker, my fourth grade teacher. You pushed me to read and write in ways that have shaped me to this day. I remember all the readings you asked me to do of my short stories, all the books you bought for me, how you let me start up a classroom newspaper. Thank you so much!

To the authors who I don't know personally but who inspire me: J. K. Rowling, for creating the series that made me love reading even more than I already did, the one that I constantly come back to when I feel lost as a reader. The author that made me realize I could do this for a living. R. L. Stine, for being a huge inspiration in this ghost story. C. S. Lewis, for inspiring me as an author and Christian. Morgan Matson, for writing really awesome books. Jenny Han—I had a ticket to see you in NYC, but it was the day Holly called and offered me representation, so I missed it. Thank you for creating Lara Jean.

Lara Willard: Four years ago I told you that I'd thank you in my acknowledgments for all your help. I haven't forgotten!

To the Bookish Community: Finding you was the push I needed to read, write, and share my love for books in the way I've always wanted. Thank you.

Lastly but certainly not least: the readers. Thank you for taking the time to read this book that I put so much into. I hope that, when reading this, between the scary moments, you realize that this is a story of hope, forgiveness, friendship, family, and love. Never give up, and never grow bitter, no matter what kind of curveballs life throws your way. Work hard, be kind, and everything else will fall into place.

Turn the page for a sneak peek at
The Girl in the Lake, another chilling
ghost story by India Hill Brown

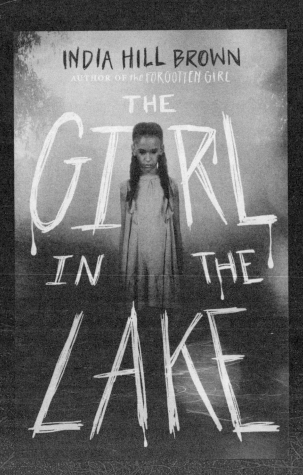

CHAPTER 1

Every time Grandma Judy or Grandad Jim called, whether it was to wish us happy birthday or Merry Christmas or just to talk with Mama, they'd always make us promise to come visit their lake house "next summer."

"Next summer" is finally here. Just a couple of weeks after I failed my last swimming lesson.

I don't think that's a coincidence, either. Grandma Judy and Grandad Jim are huge on everyone in our family loving the water and learning how to swim. So of course, when I fail my swimming lesson and decide I won't be swimming again, it's the summer we actually visit the lake house.

"You can't fail a swimming lesson, Celeste," my dad tells me after I failed it. But as a dad, he's supposed to say that. My little brother, Owen, learned really fast, but at the end of my last one, I still didn't know how to swim, which seems like failing to me.

I told my dad afterward that I don't want to swim anymore, but I should have known better than to say that.

"You know how important swimming is to our family," Mama said. Her dad, Grandad Jim, was a lifeguard. Mama says she's been swimming for so long, she doesn't even remember learning. Dad was afraid of swimming until after he married Mama, when she convinced him to finally learn, so I thought he'd understand how hard it was. But instead he says, "If I can learn, you can learn."

I think I get my swimming genes from Dad, because every time my instructor, Stinky-Breath Jared, told me to jump into his arms, I'd freeze up. Eventually, he'd get annoyed.

I did *not* like Jared with the Stinky Breath. He sighed way too many times when I wasn't brave enough to jump into his arms in the swimming pool. Like I was taking too long. But I didn't get it. For the next forty minutes, he didn't have anywhere else to be. Why was he rushing me?

He pronounced my name wrong, too. He would always say it like "Cel-es-tee." Until I worked up the nerve to correct him.

"It's Cel-*lest*," I finally told him, staring at my reflection in the rippling blue water.

"Just come on," he said. I could tell he was getting annoyed. "You can do it. It's not that hard."

I didn't have the guts to tell him that it *was* that hard for me. I wanted to tell him that my name wasn't that hard to pronounce, either, but he kept messing that up, and I'd never jumped in a body of water before. I wanted to tell him that since he seemed so annoyed with me, that I didn't trust him to catch me if I messed up. So I didn't say anything.

Just forget it, I thought to myself.

I wouldn't move an inch closer to the water. I just stood there, smelling the chlorine. One time I heard someone giggle and it was a toddler. She had on a swimsuit that was made to look like a strawberry. She was laughing at me. Then she jumped into her own daddy's arms in the pool without a care in the world.

After that last lesson, I suggested that my daddy teach me how to swim instead. I'd feel way more comfortable jumping into his arms than Stinky-Breath Jared's. Or Mama's, since she's so good at it.

"Grandad will teach you," she told me. Then she stopped herself and said, "Grandad *can* teach you." After she said this, she asked Owen and me how we'd feel about spending the week with our grandparents and cousins. And that lets me know that's the whole reason we're going to the lake house this summer.

Now I'm in the car with my mom, my dad, and Owen, on the way there. It used to be a place that my mom and her brothers and sisters would play and swim all summer long with our grandparents. Then when my grandparents stopped working, they moved there full-time. I love our grandparents, but since we moved a little farther away, we don't see them as much. Our cousins will be there, too. They are from different states and I haven't seen them in a couple of years. I just remember Capri being bossy and Daisy being quiet.

Owen must realize we're getting closer, because he finally stops telling us every single fact he knows about trees, lakes, and hiking trails and just stares out the window. If Grandma and Grandad were going to make me swim, then they were probably going to make Owen hike, too. My brainiac brother is usually totally logical, but for some reason hiking is the one thing he's really afraid of.

Our car bounces up and down on a dirt road, the trees closing in on either side of the car. I never knew a road could be so bumpy. We pass a town library, a small grocery store, and then pretty soon, I don't see much of anything except for houses every now and then.

"We're here," Mama says. She turns around and smiles at me and Owen in the back seat. I try to smile back. Mama always talks about how she and her brothers and sisters—my aunts and uncles—loved to come here and swim when they were younger. I guess she thinks it's going to be the same with me and my cousins.

We pull up to a big white house with black shutters. I can see the lake peeking out from behind the house, sparkling in the sun. It's a beautiful setting, but seeing the water makes my stomach flip. There's a window at the very top of the house—I guess it's the attic. As I'm looking, I see something shine from the attic window, like a shadow with a really bright outline. *What is that?* I wonder. It's probably just the sunlight glinting off the glass.

"There's Grandma and Grandad!" Mom exclaims happily. "And there are your cousins." She points to the group of people clustered near the door. "They can't wait to see you. And look at my brothers and sisters! Let's go say hello."

We step out of the car and stretch the achiness out of our limbs. Even though we're only about an hour away from home, it's definitely hotter here, even with the cool breeze coming from the lake. Mama can't hide her grin as she and Daddy walk over to my aunts and uncles.

I see my uncle Howard getting bags out of a car parked right in front of ours, so I guess my cousin Capri is just getting here, too.

My eyes land on Capri. Her legs are twice as long as they were the last time I saw her, and the muscles in her calves are twice as big. She'll probably be taller than Uncle Howard next year. She does not look like someone who "can't wait" to see me. She walks from behind Uncle Howard's car in some slouchy jean shorts that are just the right color blue, have the right amount of rips, aren't too tight, too loose, or too long. Her braids hang down her back and she's wearing gold hoop earrings, the really big ones that Mama won't let me wear yet. She's busy doing something on her phone and then I see her suck her teeth—probably when she realizes there is no cell phone service out here. I already realized that in the car.

Then there's my cousin Daisy. She is standing beside my aunt Marlene and uncle Steve wearing a white sundress with big red polka dots on it. She has an old-timey look, like she just stepped out of a black-and-white film. She always has—especially in her baby pictures, when she stared into the camera with her big round eyes. She has fluffy, bouncy curls and perfect posture, and looks straight ahead as she walks. Not down. Almost like she's floating through the air. I could bet money no one ever told her to "sit up straight." She's kind of old-fashioned; she likes record players and stuff. Sometimes my dad would joke and say, "She's seems like she's been here before." Whatever that means.

Owen and I walk over to them.

Daisy looks up, her hair blowing in the wind.

"Hello," she says. She is eleven, a year younger than me. She sounds so formal, like we aren't all cousins who used to play together a lot when we were little. But maybe that's just her personality.

"Hi," Owen and I say in unison.

She stares at us, taking us in. Her eyes feel like they're looking straight through me, like she can tell what I'm feeling.

"Owen and Celeste have grown a whole foot since I've seen them!" Uncle Howard's voice booms over ours as he laughs. He looks and sounds just like Grandad.

"Haven't they? And look at Capri's long legs! They will definitely get that Hawthorne height, that's for sure," Mama says, laughing as she hugs her brother.

"I've heard you've learned how to swim, Owen!" Howard slaps Owen on the back as a sign of congratulations.

Owen smiles a little, glancing at me before he says, "Yeah."

"Don't worry, Celeste. Between that beautiful lake and the pool up the road, you'll be swimming in no time. Maybe Capri can drive you—"

Mama clears her throat and Capri glares at her dad. Then she glares at me. *What did I do?* Uncle Howard is sweating as if he's said something he shouldn't say. Or maybe he's sweating because it's so hot out here.

"Daisy, I love your dress," my mom says, trying to change the subject.

"Thank you," she says. She does a curtsy, like a girl out of a fairy tale book, and Capri scoffs while Owen and I look at each other. Who does that?

"This girl. Straight out of the past," Aunt Marlene says. She gives Daisy's shoulder a squeeze. "All she ever wants to do is listen to her records and watch black-and-white movies."

We stand there as our parents talk and laugh with our aunts and uncles for a while, then they say their goodbyes.

"Have the best time," Mama says, giving Owen and then me a huge hug. She and Dad look genuinely sad to go. Maybe they should stay here and us kids should go back to our houses, since they have so much fun here.

"My girl. Call me if you need anything," Dad says. He winks, and somehow I know he's talking about swimming. Dad was afraid of swimming before he met Mom, he told me. So I think he gets it. But it's not that I'm afraid of swimming, exactly. At first it sounded fun, but my swimming instructor made it kind of difficult for me, and now I just don't care anymore. Maybe he was right, it wasn't that hard, and I was just being silly. And not to mention, right after failing, I had a nightmare about falling into a big body of water. It felt so real and now I'm definitely not in a big rush to learn how to swim.

"Okay," I say, hugging him, too.

Capri walks over to us, a scowl on her face. Daisy, Owen, and I all say hi to her, but she just waves us off. I sigh. I don't want to have to deal with her attitude all week. I always thought Capri was pretty bossy, anyway. I don't get it. When I'm at home, I'm the oldest and I don't boss Owen around at all.

We wave as the grown-ups pile into their cars and then disappear, one by one, until all that's left is an old Ford pickup truck and a Jeep. Grandma and Grandad's cars.

I peek around the back of the house to the wide, green backyard. The trees have branches that hang really low and create long shadows across the grass. They back into a wooded area that looks worn down with tire tracks. I wonder if Grandad drives through there to get through town. I wonder if that's where Grandma and Grandad hike. I wonder what's back there.

I look around some more. I see the deck that leads to the lake.

I can't help but admit to myself that the lake is beautiful, with its deep blue and the glitter from the sun. But it's so big, it overwhelms me. It's at least ten times bigger than the pool. Will Grandad make me jump in the lake? I hope not. It's pretty to look at, but the thought of jumping in makes me feel dizzy.

Owen, Capri, Daisy, and I stand in an awkward silence for a second, staring at the house, the sparkling lake behind it.

"Come on in," Grandma says. She has a wide smile and nose like Mom.

We walk into the house and it's like all the hot air outside is packed into it. My forehead is still sweaty from standing outside. It smells different from our house. It makes a lot of noises, too, lots of creaks and groans. As soon as I walk in, the house sighs really loudly, it almost sounds like a voice saying "*Hiiii.*" We all stare at the ceiling. Grandma must see our expressions, because she tells us that it's just the "house settling in," whatever that means.

"All of your rooms are upstairs," Grandma says. "You can choose the ones you want and unpack, then come back downstairs for supper."

I already know which one I want: the one with the best view of the lake. Just because I don't want to swim in it doesn't mean I don't want to draw the view.

I run upstairs and into the room on the far left, eager to get the one with the biggest balcony before Capri does. The sun is setting just outside my window, the big oak tree casting a shadow over a room that looks like a big hand.

The floor creaks when I step inside, like the rest of this house. The bed looks comfortable, though, and there is a huge colorful quilt on the bed. The only things in here are a nightstand, a lamp, a dresser, the bed, and the quilt. I decide to put some things around the room, to make it feel more like home since it will be my home for the next week. I put a picture that my friends and I took at my friend Iris's summer slumber party on the dresser with my sketch pad and colored pencils right beside it.

I told Iris about Stinky-Breath Jared, and how he made me feel. She told me that I should've told him right then and there.

"You should've told him just like this!" she said, standing up with her beaded braids clanking together. "'First of all, my name is *Celeste*. I've never swum before and that's why it's hard. Duh! And your stinky breath isn't making it any easier. Stop acting annoyed with me and be patient!' And then when you did jump in, you could've splashed him," She giggled at the last part.

I just laughed and shook my head. I'm not like Iris. Sometimes it's hard for me to say what I feel.

I unroll my picture of Simone Manuel, the Olympic gold medalist swimmer, and stick it on the wall with a roll of tape I found at the bottom of my bag. I hope that she will inspire me to gather up the nerve to at least jump in the pool this summer.

I look around the room and try to get used to it. Even though it's so old, it still feels new to me. And quiet. And hot. The warm air is so thick, it makes the room feel crowded, like someone is in here with me. I look around, twice, even though I know I'm the only person in here. I open a window to let some air in.

I hear a knock at the door. "It's time for dinner," someone says, and then I hear feet running away. The voice is strangely old-fashioned—Daisy, I guess.

"Coming," I call. I go back into the hallway, the floor still creaking under my feet.

The door slams behind me.

I jump. Then I remember I left the window open. Sometimes at home when I leave the window open, my bedroom door slams, too.

I hear low giggling behind one of the doors and stop for a second to listen. It's probably Daisy again. Or maybe Capri got her phone to work.

I shake my head. I keep stopping and looking around at random things. I just need to let myself get used to this house and new-to-me bedroom.

I walk downstairs. When I reach the door to the kitchen, I see everyone in the house is already sitting at the dinner table, settled in.

That's weird, I think. Then who's upstairs laughing? I guess it's just more creaking noises from this old lake house.

"Oh, Celeste! That's funny, I thought you were already down here." Grandma furrows her brows together, looking around at the dinner table, as if she sees me sitting there.

"Me too," says Daisy. She looks at the same empty seat that Grandma looks at.

"I was upstairs, starting to unpack," I say, sitting in the chair between Daisy and Owen. I look at Daisy. "I thought . . ." But I don't finish because Grandma is placing the last dish on the table.

Grandma looks around at us and smiles. "Who's hungry? I made a big dinner and a pitcher of fresh lemonade for us to enjoy."

My stomach growls in response. I hold Daisy's and Owen's hands as Grandad leads grace. After we say amen, I help myself to the dinner spread around the table and try to decide what to start with. I pick up an ear of sweet corn and bite into it.

"Capri, I hear congratulations are in order," Grandad says, a twinkle in his eye.

Capri looks up, her frown replaced by surprise.

"Your father told me you're the new track team captain!"

"Thanks." She smiles, but then frowns again, like she just remembered something. She goes back to eating her food.

"Y'all eat up and sleep good tonight," Grandad says, looking around the table at us. He is super tall with a big booming voice and a gray beard. I haven't seen that smile in a little while, but I've missed it. "There's so much for us to do this week!"

"Like what?" Capri grumbles. Her phone is lying beside her on the table, untouched. I guess she gave up on trying to get cell service. There's no Wi-Fi here, either.

"Why, all types of things!" Grandad opens his arms wide, his voice getting loud across the table. "For starters, we have a lake. Good for boating and swimming!"

He looks at me and winks. I smile back and put my head down, a little embarrassed. I know I'm the only person at the table who can't swim. I just know that Mama set this trip up so I could learn.

Owen clears his throat. "A boy at school told me that he never knew Black people had their own lake houses and he didn't believe me when I said you had one. He still thought I was making it up. I can't wait to show him photos of this place when I get back home."

I take another bite out of my corn on the cob, trying to stay silent, but the crunch is too loud. I glare at Owen, trying to get him to stop talking about swimming and water, but once he gets started, he can't be stopped.

He's still babbling. "He said it doesn't make sense for us to have our own lake houses because most Black people can't . . . swim." And that's when he looks up at me and gives me an apologetic smile.

Too late now, Owen. I continue eating my corn on the cob.

Grandad takes a bite of chicken and wipes his mouth off with his napkin. He looks straight at Owen. "You tell that fellow to learn his history. There's a reason a lot of Black people don't know how to swim. There was a time where Black people weren't even allowed in public pools. Do you all know the famous actress Dorothy Dandridge?"

Owen shakes his head, Capri shrugs with a frown, and Daisy gasps. "Oh, I love her!" she says. She's so quiet, I'd almost forgotten she's here.

"She was a legendary entertainer. And legend has it that an entire pool was drained at a Las Vegas hotel that she was supposed to perform at, because she stuck her toe in it. Can you imagine?"

"So Black people can't swim because they wouldn't let Dorothy Dandridge stick her foot in a pool at a hotel?" Capri asks, still frowning. I stare at her. I wonder what her problem is. She acts tough, but I can tell she really wants to know.

"It's more than that," Grandma says. "Once, Dr. King was arrested for integrating a restaurant at a motel. Peaceful protesters decided to wade into the motel pool to support him. Do you know that the pool owner poured acid in the pool while the protesters were inside of it?" She shakes her head. Owen's eyes are wide. I know he can't wait to tell his friends this later.

"When my sister and I were younger, so many pools had Whites Only signs on them," Grandma continues. "How could we possibly learn to swim? If we tried at all, we had to swim in rivers and that could be dangerous. Years of not being allowed in pools or having the police being called on us for simply *being* in a pool, we rarely had the opportunity to learn. So we weren't able to pass that knowledge, or the simple joy of having fun in the water on the weekends, to our kids. All we could pass was the fear of the water or getting in trouble for something we just wanted to enjoy. So your classmate was right, in a way, that many Black people can't swim. But it's important that you know why, and that we work to change that. After Ellie—"

She stops, looks at Grandad, and sticks her fork into her macaroni and cheese. The sudden pause makes all of us look up, including Capri.

"Ellie?" Capri asks.

"Celestine. Your great-aunt Ellie," Grandma says.

"Oh," I say. That's who I'm named after. My full name is Celeste Anne Cooper. I love my name because it's fun to draw lots of swirls around the *C*'s and the *E*'s. My great-aunt was named Celestine Johnson. I know that everyone called her Ellie for short, but I don't have a nickname. I'm just Celeste. I'm reminded again of the swimming instructor—always getting my name wrong, then asking me to jump in the pool. How could I trust someone to catch me when they couldn't even pronounce my name right?

"What about Great-Aunt Ellie?" Owen asks.

"Nothing, baby." Grandma shakes her head. I know she died when Grandma was younger. I guess it still hurts for her to talk about her.

"Your grandmother wanted to make it her duty to get her entire family swimming," Grandad continues. "That's how we met, you know. I was a lifeguard at the local community pool and she came to learn. Love at first swim." They exchange a smile.

I'm still eating all this good food, but I can't help but feel a little guilty. All Grandma's ever wanted is for her grandchildren to learn how to swim, and here I am, failing at swimming lessons.

"You look just like her. You know that?" Grandma says. I look up and she's staring right at me.

"Me?" I glance at Owen and he shrugs.

Grandma is still staring at me and I don't know what to say. I've never even seen a picture of Great-Aunt Ellie before, so I don't know if I really look like her. People say I look like Owen, but we only have the same eyes, Mom's hazel-brown eyes. Otherwise, I don't see it.

It's like Grandma reads my mind, because she asks me if I'd like to see a picture of her.

"I'll bring out the photo album after dinner," Grandma says. She wipes her mouth with a napkin and a smile. "She's the reason your grandfather built this place for me."

As the conversation moves on, I finish my food. I'm stuffed and ready for the first night in my new bed. Grandma puts a sweet potato pie on the table for dessert, but I don't know if I can eat a bite more. Owen, of course, takes a piece and puts it on one of the small dishes Grandma brought out.

Grandma disappears and comes back with a big black book. She wipes some crumbs off the table before she gently places it down. Grandad steps behind Grandma and looks over her shoulder. Daisy scoots her chair closer to the table and Capri leans in.

We flip through some pictures I've seen copies of before, of my mom and aunts and uncles, running around under fire hydrants, playing in the pool, diving off the diving board, fishing and smiling in canoes.

Grandma smiles really big, looks at me, and hands me the photo album. "There she is. My big sister Celestine," she says. "Have a look."

I look, ready to say something polite about how pretty she is or how nice she probably was. But when I see the picture, I scream. My heart beats fast and I hear Owen yell, Daisy squeal, and even Capri gasps.

I'm looking at a picture of myself.